Subhas Death That Wasn't

A. K. GANDHI

PRABHAT PRAKASHAN

Published by
PRABHAT PRAKASHAN PVT. LTD.
4/19 Asaf Ali Road,
New Delhi-110002 (INDIA)
e-mail: prabhatbooks@gmail.com

ISBN 978-93-5521-839-1
SUBHAS DEATH THAT WASN'T
by A. K. Gandhi

Edition
First, 2023

Price
₹ 250 (Rupees Two Hundred Fifty Only)

Printed at
Japan Art, Delhi

It is a book of historical fiction and any similarity with any person, dead or alive, is a mere coincidence.

Author's Note

In modern times, we have remained hooked to numerous mysteries that have kept people confounded; in most cases, the veracity of facts and arguments presented has been far from satisfactory. One of the most intriguing mysteries pertains to the death of Netaji Subhas Chandra Bose, the legendary leader whom the countrymen adore so dearly; his survival or death remains completely shrouded in mystery.

It is no easy task to comprehend the life of a great man of his stature, as it is often filled to the brim with twists and turns, triumphs and tribulations, leaving behind a rich legacy for the masses to relish forever. When it comes to a leader like Bose, his accomplishments have left people in awe and admiration.

The mystery behind his death, or rather life, however, has taken the form of a controversy as one faction is reluctant to give in to the other's viewpoint. The numerous committees and commissions have failed to unearth the truth as conflicting evidences and viewpoints together with the fear of international relations going sour, have hindered a conclusive inference on part of the government. Even the release of Bose's files in the public domain has not helped to resolve the issue.

It is in the wake of uncertainty engulfing this matter that different theories have been presented, but no one has ever dared to look at this mystery the way this book does, as other theories tend to hide more than they reveal. The theory professed by this book goes on to reveal that there is more to the mystery than what we have been made to believe. This is sure that had this enigmatic personality lived on, the history of the country post-independence would have been quite different.

The present book does not limit itself to resolving this mystery in its own unique way, it also lays bare the convictions and beliefs that have been associated with his life and decisions, in essence appearing equally mysterious like his death, including his relations with Gandhiji. It also convincingly deals with his survival theories, like that of Gumnami Baba in Faizabad (Ayodhya) and others, to bring out the truth.

The book is also about the enduring rich legacy that this leader has left behind, helping people to be inspired by his mind-boggling adventures and thought-provoking ideas, and how he lived and sacrificed for his ideals and freedom.

This book is only a humble tribute to the great soul with an insightful vision to resolve the mystery. A lot of study and research have gone into this book, and I am sure this would set to rest the controversy; it will prove to be a book worth reading in one sitting. I owe gratitude to all those scholars and historians whose guidance and works have guided me to arrive at my conclusions.

Contents

The Escape

January 18, 1941. Subhas Chandra Bose was still in the dress that he wore while escaping from house arrest in Calcutta: Aligarhi pyjama and black long coat. His grand personality looked still better with the black cap on his head and the round glasses on his eyes. He eagerly waited at the Gomoh railway station, while Sisir and Amiya Nath, his nephews, stood at a little distance. They would glance at each other and anxiously wait for the train to arrive. Bose stood near the boundary wall, just near the bush planted on the platform, so that he would not be visible so easily.

As Bose carefully scanned the platform, he found a pair of eyes staring at him. He felt uncomfortable. Was his secrecy out? Was he a detective of the British government? If it were so, his escape could be jeopardised, he thought keenly. Was his escape found out? He had planned such that his escape would not come to notice for at least a week, and he was not yet away for one day.

No one but Bose knew the entire plan; Sisir and Amiya Nath knew that he was to take Delhi-Kalka Mail, but had no idea where he was destined to go. He had kept the entire plan under wraps.

Quickly looking around, Bose once again looked to that direction in which a pair of eyes was staring at him. Yes, he found the man still gazing at him. Oh! And then he assured himself that the path he had chosen to tread was a thorny one; service to motherland was no easy task; all types of dangers had to be faced and overcome; he was ready to confront any type of dangers that could come up. He had overcome several impediments during his life ever since he dedicated himself to the country's freedom; and now he was on his greatest mission, and did not want it to be aborted just for some foolish mistake.

Bose kept standing where he was. The train was behind schedule by a few minutes. The pair of eyes had made him somewhat uncomfortable, but it could be his doubt too. He commanded a fascinating personality, and it was no extraordinary for people to stick their gaze at him, he had experienced this situation even before. He was a popular leader and thousands of people waited at his call. But since he was on a secret mission now, he had to be extra cautious. His secret mission being divulged would be a great jolt to his entire plan.

Bose feigned to take a little walk up and down, but his intention was clear. He wanted to have a closer look at the man whose eyes had been fixed on him. As he turned to the right and took a few steps, he could not find the man. This could mean two things. 'If I have been found out, he must have gone to fetch the force,' murmured Bose to himself, 'or in the alternative, he was just another passenger or maybe someone who had come to the railway station to see off or receive someone and had found him curious for some reason.'

There were not many people on the platform. Bose once again took his place that was near the boundary wall, very near a bush, which was helping him to ward off several glances. He did not want any one to notice him, even in his camouflage. At some distance, he noticed some British army officers with their families. Maybe they were about to board the same train.

Bose heaved a sigh of relief when the train whistled in. Feeling the ticket in his coat pocket, he picked up his bag and holdall and headed towards the compartment. Before climbing in, he looked around. He found Sisir and Amiya Nath shaking their heads very slowly. He also looked for the man whose gaze had made him uncomfortable; he was nowhere to be found.

There were hardly ten passengers in the compartment. Bose took a seat in the second cabin, second from the window, and set his luggage under his seat. He was all alone on the berth; opposite him sat a young Sikh man. 'This is just fine,' he said to himself.

Until the train moved, Bose kept looking out of the window every few seconds. As the train started, he leaned back, and as he was about to close his eyes, he saw the same man on the platform rushing towards the train; he had only a small cloth bag in his right hand. 'Is he really after me?' Bose grew restless. He moved towards the edge of his seat to be able to see any people entering the compartment. Nobody had entered the compartment. But he was no more at rest. 'It could be my fancy, but I have to be careful.'

The train had picked up speed. The fields and trees were rushing back. He shut the window as the cold air made him shiver. Seeing him downing the window, the Sikh too rose and shut his window.

"Where are you going?" asked the Sikh co-passenger.

"Just where the train will take," Bose was unwilling to start a dialogue. He knew from his experience that Punjabis are very loud and talkative, and he did not want any one to pay untoward attention to him.

But the Sikh passenger wanted to strike a familiarity. "What is your name? I am Harveer Singh."

"Maulvi Ziauddin," said Bose briefly. Leaning back he closed his eyes, so no conversation would take place.

So far everything had materialised as per the plan, but that strange man had caused him some anxiety. Maybe there could be some problem at the next station, he thought, and then he shirked his ideas. He wanted a brief rest. He wanted to ponder over his present actions. He slowly closed his eyes.

The past two years had been very exciting. Some events had rapidly occurred during this period that had changed the very course of his life. It was largely this period that had necessitated this journey, which was going to be long, tiresome and full of dangers.

Bose recalled the words he had uttered while assuming the post of the President of the Indian National Congress in 1938 at Haripura Session : "Some friends in the Congress think that the Congress should be dissolved after independence. This is a misleading notion, because the party which would beget the country's freedom, would have to implement the work of its reconstruction too; it would have to bear the burden of administration. If the Congress is forcibly ended, it would end continuity. After freedom, the Congress will have to play three types of roles: to prepare the country for relinquishing selfish interests; to make efforts for India's unity and national integration; and accord provincial and cultural rights."

However, Gandhiji wanted that the Congress should be dissolved after independence. Bose had some difference of opinions with Gandhiji, but this was a point on which the two completely differed; and some more decisions on his part were going to set his path apart from that of the Congress. Gandhiji wanted cottage industry to become a tool for national reconstruction and development, but Bose knew that only industrialisation was the key to development and progress in the modern world. However, this point was only the tip of the iceberg.

The most important point on which they differed was the way the national movement for freedom was to be conducted. They were like fire and water, which could not stay together. Gandhiji was a moderate leader who was a votary of nonviolence. He believed in confrontation through Satyagraha, fasting and other peaceful means. Bose, on the other hand, believed in the concept of self-sacrifice. He could go to the extent of putting his life to peril for the sake of his solemn goal. From his actions, he never seemed to act in contravention to Gandhiji's policies, but he never supported them either. His experiences in life had helped him lay down his peculiar ideologies and policies; his principles were not based on any extreme ideology; he could transform them as per the need of the hour. He was not in the favour of extremism, but at the same time, he believed that armed revolution was not improper under the prevailing circumstances. He expressed once that the government should be convinced about the country's demands with folded hands, which the moderates had been doing, but the same hands should be turned into fists if those demands were not met; it was only the most vigorous method to make Indians feel their strength. He wanted the Indian people to become aware of the fact that they were capable of giving the message of love, harmony and peace; and if needed, they could change their tactics to use might to any extent.

In 1937, Japan had attacked China, and the prevailing circumstances and expanding hostilities in the world had made it almost certain that the Second World War was round the corner. This had become quite clear towards the end of Bose's term as the President of the Congress in 1938. He pondered over the entire situation deeply. He had seen how the British had tricked Indians into supporting them in the First World War. He came to the conclusion that the British government should be warned that they should free India if they wanted our cooperation in the war. Moreover, he also wanted to give out a warning to the British that they could have to face an armed rebellion in case they did not heed to this demand.

Gandhiji, however, was not in agreement with his view. According to him, this thinking was in contravention of the 'idealistic nonviolent policy' that the Congress had decided to follow. It was owing to Gandhiji's opposition to this view that the Congress members rejected this idea completely.

This was how two doctrines, poles apart from each other, worked in the Congress. It led to conflict of ideas, creating a wider divide between the two.

The train was losing speed as its noise changed pitch. Maybe the next station is approaching, Bose thought. With this thought, he became alert. He was sunk deep in his thoughts, but had not lost sight of the mysterious pair of eyes. He readied himself for any eventuality. He opened the window and looked out. The train was passing through an open field. A small town was visible at a distance. How peaceful the entire country looks, but it is boiling within, he thought.

The train came to halt. He was alert, but did not want to show this change in his gesture. He continued to sit leaning his back on the seat. He kept an eye on the passengers who boarded the compartment. There were not many people. Just two passengers boarded.

Bose felt relieved when the train whistled and moved ahead. He downed the window, and once again closed his eyes.

During his house arrest, he had meditated a lot and formed his ideas. But in this train, he could not meditate because he was in the dress of a Muslim gentleman, and it could have given someone a basis for suspicion. This could be disastrous, so he had to be careful to ward off any suspicion.

The past events were passing before his eyes like a fleeting panorama. Bose had received a great acclaim; he had won people's confidence in his policies. The decisions that he took during one year of his tenure at the high post had made him still more popular. He was now known throughout the country. His popularity was often compared with that of Gandhiji, much ahead that of Jawaharlal Nehru, Sardar Patel and others.

In December 1938, the Congress was getting ready for another annual session, this time it was decided that it would be held in Tripura. Bose pondered over what he should do, and in view of his popularity, he decided to contest the election. However, he was well aware that Gandhiji, the axis of the entire Congress, was opposed to him. Gandhiji wanted to nominate Nehru, but he had already become the President thrice, so he could not be nominated. Gandhiji selected Maulana Abul Kalam Azad as the next candidate, saying that this step could cultivate trust in the Muslim community, but he expressed inability owing to ill-health. This was how Dr. Pattabhi Sitaramayya was made the next candidate.

Bose had made up his mind to contest the election, but he knew that his difference of opinions with Gandhiji was sure to bring him in open confrontation. He had already received support from several provincial Congress committees, but the national working committee supported Sitaramayya. The prominent leaders, including Sardar Vallabhbhai Patel, Rajendra Prasad, Jairamdas, J.B. Kripalani, Daulatram, Jamnalal Bajaj, Shankardev Rao and Bhulabhai Desai, issued a statement which said: "The election to the President of the Congress has traditionally been held unopposed. Unless there prevail special circumstances, an individual, who has been on this post, is not permitted to contest for this post. In view of these facts, Bose should clear the path for Sitaramayya."

Bose could read between the lines. He refused to withdraw his name and decided to contest the election. He said in support of his ideas, "This matter is not personal. Our struggle against imperialism has led to cultivation of new ideas, new thinking, new ideals, new principles, new programmes and new problems. People think that the election of the Congress President should be above limited problems and programmes, it should be based on people's aspirations and expectations. I am unaware of any such rule as per which an individual cannot contest election more than once. If you looked at Congress's history, you would know it clearly. It has occurred several times before. Moreover, the election to this post is held with common concurrence. Several provinces have nominated me for this post without my knowledge. They have urged that I should continue on this post. The Indian masses have supported this. I have not received even a single suggestion that goes against this idea. However, if a dedicated Congressman like Narendra Dev is ready to assume the command of the Congress, I would willingly withdraw my name, else it would be decided in the meeting to be held on 29 January."

The matter had come to a head. Nobody had ever imagined that any one could go against Gandhiji's wishes, but it was also sure that Bose could not win without Gandhiji's support.

Bose's experiences had made him a master strategist. Opposing Gandhiji was no child's play. He had to act like Abhimanyu. He knew that, like Abhimanyu, he might not be able to pierce through all the garrisons, but he was sure that he would be able to pierce most of them. The only national party of the country had been divided vertically into two groups – one was behind Bose while the other stood firmly behind Gandhiji.

Even before the ballots started to be counted on 29 January, 1941, Bose had a lovely smile on his lips. His confidence even at this crucial point showed that he was not that Abhimanyu who had to sacrifice himself at the final exit; he was once again making himself ready to take up the cudgels of the party and lead the national movement from the front. People watched the counting of votes with bated breath, and when the result was declared, everybody pressed their fingers between their teeth. Bose had defeated Sitaramayya by a comfortable margin of 200 votes. The entire country was amazed. It was defeat, not of Sitaramayya, but that of Gandhiji. Bose had proved that he was Arjun, and not Abhimanyu. No one had until then dared to challenge Gandhiji; who was so desperate that he stated that Dr. Sitaramayya's defeat was in fact his own.

Gandhiji further shocked the country when he indicated his retirement from the Congress. It was on his hint that the members of the working committee handed over their letters of resignation.

Bose was agitated at this unethical conduct. It was like undermining his election. He did not want any direct confrontation with Gandhiji, despite his difference of opinions. He immediately issued a statement saying that his sole aim was to regain Gandhiji's confidence. He met Gandhiji and tried to assuage the feelings, with a request for the members' support, but Gandhiji was firm. He expressed his inability and suggested that he should form a new working committee. It was evident that he was in no mood to compromise. Bose had to return disappointed.

Bose also found the tide slowly turning against him in the Congress, because Gandhiji had hinted at his retirement, and this could blunt the sharp edge of the national movement. Bose wanted to work in the national interest. For him, individual gains were of no importance, so he made up his mind to choose a separate path for himself. This could well be in the favour of the national movement, as his individual effort could create yet another front for the British to contend with, who were already finding it somewhat difficult to deal with the Congress.

The Congress Working Committee meeting was held in March. At this time, Bose was seriously ill, yet he attended it, though on a stretcher. The stalwart leader, Govind Ballabh Pant moved a resolution by which confidence was expressed in the older working committee and selection of its members as per Gandhiji's wish was proposed. The resolution was passed by majority. The supporters of this resolution also included some of those members who had supported Bose in his election, but they were possibly scared of the outcome that could arise after Gandhiji's retirement. The entire process was a mockery of the democratic principles that the Congress showed itself to be a supporter of.

It was complete injustice. It was a sort of disrespect to Bose, it was simply unacceptable to him, so he decided to resign from his post. Submitting his resignation on 29 April, 1939, he stated that the new working committee would find it difficult to function under his supervision, so it was free to choose any other person as the President. He expressed hope that his resignation would be in the best interests of the country and the national movement, and would also do away with the non-cooperative atmosphere that had been created.

The Congress immediately accepted his resignation. The Congress members might have been happy at their success, but the people did not take it lightly. It was like a blot on its face, because even today, in the present twenty-first century, this point is discussed casting aspersions on the democratic norms in the Congress. The newspapers too did not take this conspiracy lightly. People showed their support for the ousted leader. Even Rabindranath Tagore expressed his sentiments in favour of Bose in a long article. He also wrote letters to Gandhiji and Nehru asking them to strike a compromise, but to no avail. The divide seemed to have widened.

This incident was like a paradigm shift for Bose. He opened his eyes to look around. The train was moving at its scheduled speed. Finding everything normal around, he closed his eyes. He did not find the strange pair of eyes anywhere near him. This must be because of his over-cautious mind that assigned so much importance to that stranger, thought he. Once again, he sank in the recent past. It was like introspection, it could tell him if he was on the right path, if his decision to do what he was going to do was right or not, justifiable or not. He knew he was going to create history, but would the progeny accept his actions because he was about to take an untrodden path.

Despite his resignation, Bose had high hopes with the Congress, as it alone seemed the instrument that could further the cause of freedom, so he did not want to quit it. At that time, it was the only national-level organisation which could make some difference, though it was not inclined in the right direction, Bose felt. At the same time, Bose felt that people in the Congress were trying to look down upon him or undermine his popularity. They thought that he would be left alone in the wilderness after he was no more in any authority in the Congress, but Bose was cast from a different type of fabric. He was no wax statue that could melt upon a little heat; he was born to be a rock that would remain firm despite all the earthquakes that could be brought upon to wreak havoc on him.

For Bose, nothing less than Swaraj or self-rule could be acceptable, and after all the atrocities unleashed by the British, use of armed resistance was quite justifiable. He had to prove himself to the people that he might have been down, but he was certainly not out. Just three days after his resignation, he declared his intention to form the All India Forward Bloc. It was to be a faction within the Congress. He stated that this Bloc would infuse life in the dormant energy of the Congress, and was meant to stir the national movement for freedom. He expressed his intention that it would initiate its movement for complete freedom as soon as favourable conditions dawned.

With this declaration, his leftist leanings were becoming explicit. He supported socialism, like Nehru, but he differed from him so far as the degree of his doctrine went. He wanted to eradicate all types of discriminations and self-interests for the sake of social, economic and political equanimity. He had foreseen the danger of religion mixing with politics, so he warned against it from the very outset; he had found its traces in the Congress. He was also opposed to regionalism as well as reeling corruption among the Congressmen owing to their inclination for the power. He wanted the Congress to emerge as a lively and dynamic organisation free from selfish interests.

The All India Forward Bloc became popular in his home province of Bengal in no time and people became its volunteers in large numbers. It was gaining popularity in the other provinces too, but in Madras, he himself witnessed how popular his new organisation had become.

A votary of armed conflict, Bose did not want to create eternal enmity with the British. Despite their atrocities and his wish to throw them out of the country, he was deeply impressed by their methodical and systematic approach and steadfast disciplinarian outlook towards life. He was aware that 90 percent of India's population was illiterate, so he thought that socialist authoritarianism, for a maximum period of two decades, was the answer to put India on the path to rapid development and progress.

The world scenario was quite volatile at this time. The world war could break out any moment. If Britain had availed opportunities to occupy our vast territories and repress our opportunities, it was right to repay it in its own coin. When it was to be under the stress of the war, further pressure had to be put on it to force it to concede freedom for India and other colonies. This in no way could be called immoral. And it would be equally just to take help of the powers that were in confrontation with Britain. Bose wanted to avail this opportunity, but the Congress seemed to assume a delaying tactic. In such a case, it was not clear what stance it would take in the instance the world war broke out.

Bose was becoming increasingly disenchanted with the Congress. He also felt that some disciplinary action could be taken against him any time, so he was making himself ready to embrace the new situation.

Bose conducted the all-India conference of the Forward Bloc and set his priorities. He was very concerned about development of human resource, especially the youth, who could participate in the country's progress. He opined that in the first stage of the national movement, the British would be opposed; and in the second stage, inter-party and intra-party differences would be sorted out under the overall leadership of the Congress, for a broader objective of complete social, economic and political equality and harmony.

The increasing popularity of Bose was indigestible to the Congress leaders; they wanted to clip his wings; but they adopted a step that was replete with superiority complex.

A few days after Bose's all-India conference, the Congress held its session, in which two resolutions were passed against the leftists, in their absence. This naturally angered Bose. He declared to observe a protest day on 9 July, 1939, simply overlooking the warning issued by the Congress. The entire country witnessed protests and processions in huge numbers, infuriating the Congress further. The same day, the Congress Working Committee suspended Bose from the Congress on grounds that his actions were in contravention of party discipline. It also decided that Bose could not be a member or President of the Congress for three years.

Bose was mentally ready for this sort of action. He was unhappy that the Congress had gone down to the level of playing vindictive politics against its own member, rather than taking some concrete action against the British, against whom the prevailing situations presented a unique opportunity. The cause of the country's freedom seemed to have been lost, but Bose could not allow it to happen so. He started publication of a weekly called Forward Bloc to oppose the prevailing Congress policies as well as the arrogant tendencies of the British government.

Bose wanted to start a national movement so that the British government would find it exceedingly difficult to hold on to India, because the British would find India very advantageous in the imminent war, as they could get massive manpower as well as resources from here, and Bose wanted to deprive them of this vital source. He was right too! Why should the British get to utilise our resources for the war that was rooted in imperialism, and India was a victim to it. Very ironically, Britain would declare India a party to the war in the name of fighting for the high ideals of democracy and liberty, but it was curbing these very rights in India and other colonies under its thumb.

Bose wanted Gandhiji to take steps so that Indian resources would not be used in the war, but Gandhiji seemed unwilling to do so. The Congress too seemed to sit like a duck, it was not making any noticeable effort to start a national movement for independence. So, Bose decided to take up the cudgels himself.

On 3 July, 1940, Bose decided to observe Siraj-ud-Daulah Day in the memory of the Nawab of Bengal. He also decided to demolish the Holwell Monument, built in the memory of those who had died in the Black Hole of Calcutta incident in 1756. Named so after a survivor and built in around 1901, this monument was erected in the memory of the European people who were imprisoned by Siraj-ud-Daulah in the small dungeon, where 123 of them allegedly died of suffocation.

Bose was immediately arrested and imprisoned. He was charged under sections which could lead to his life imprisonment, but his subsequent election to the Central Legislative Assembly caused these sections to be suspended. The trial too progressed at a turtle's pace, and Bose was getting impatient, especially due to the fact that the Second World War had already broken out on 1 September, 1939, and he thought that it was an opportunity that India should avail itself of. The Congress was evidently not doing anything other than opposing India being made a party to the war; but as per Bose, this was not at all enough. Much more effort needed to be made, but the Congress did not seem prepared for it.

The more ferocious the war grew, the still more impatient did Bose grow. He found it hard to breathe as a prisoner while the motherland needed him. He needed to take some urgent steps, but there was no one to listen to him. The British attention was totally deviated to the war. Bose thought how he could draw the government's attention, and he had a clue, it was to put himself at risk. On 29 November, 1940, he started his fast unto death, successfully drawing the British attention to him.

Bose was not very sound physically; he had contacted tuberculosis on an earlier occasion when he was lodged in jail in Mandalay in 1920s, and he suffered from other ailments too. The fast unto death could deal a blow to him, which would bring the entire country to a storm, and at this crucial time, the British were not prepared to face a popular uprising. They released him on 5 December, 1940, and put him under the house arrest in his own house.

The British put several restrictions on his movements within the house. He was asked not to go near the boundary wall or windows, but Bose was scarcely bothered. He limited himself to his room, grew his beard and meditated; he did not want the detectives to know that he was growing a beard. The entry of outsiders was limited to a great deal, but Bose had avenues to plan his escape. He spread rumours that he was inclined to become a Sanyasi or hermit, and the British detectives were convinced to this fact, especially in view of his conflict with Gandhiji.

Bose took inspiration for his escape from the words of Savarkar who had once said to him that a daring and enterprising young man like him should go out of India and should drive out the enemy with help from the forces on the other side. Bose had assented to this view, only he was to seek avenues to realise this intention. And now the time was not far.

The Second World War was on and was growing terrible, more terrible with each passing day. More and more countries were joining on the side of the Allied or Axis forces. The Allied forces mainly comprised Britain and France, with America until then engaged in the war effort to the extent of supplying arms. It was confronted with the Axis forces mainly comprising Germany, Italy and Japan. All this while, Germany had signed a treaty of friendship with Russia, and it was enjoying the fruit of this association to some extent. Naturally, Bose could not seek help from any country fighting a war on the side of Britain, so he had to go for one of the Axis powers, however vicious they might be. After all, an enemy of the enemy is your friend, and as he popularly said that a poison could be killed with a poison.

Bose planned his escape meticulously in conjunction with his comrades: Niranjan Singh, a member of the Forward Bloc; Sardar Baldev Singh, a trader of Jamshedpur; Sardar Achhar Singh, a member of the Kirti Kisan Party; Comrade Ram Kishan and Comrade Bhagat Ram.

The plan for escape was implemented on the night 16-17 January, 1941. He set out in his family car with his nephew Sisir, the son of his elder brother Sarat, on the driving seat. He travelled overnight to Dhanbad, stayed with Amiya Nath, his nephew, and took the Frontier Express in the evening.

So far everything had materialised as per the plan, he was a little anxious about the pair of eyes. He was not sure if this man could be a source of trouble. He could not take any untoward action unless he was certain that he was in a trouble. The train was now slowing down; he opened the window, it was pitch dark outside, cold puffs of air invaded the cabin. He was about to shut the window when he restrained himself, he wanted to confirm whether that strange man was out to keep an eye on him.

When the train slowed down, Bose looked out. Light on the platform was not sufficient, it was as good as dark. Only a few bulbs were glowing, and then he saw the man walking along the compartment, looking into the window. When he found Bose looking intently at him, he turned his face away. Bose could not see him well, but his doubt now started to turn into assurance. Still, he kept patient. It was for the first time that Bose had seen closely how he looked. He was tall, well-built and strong, like Bose himself. He could not be seen again until the train started.

It was cold, and as he was thinking what all he could do in case of a trouble, he scanned the compartment. To his relief, he found Comrade Ahmed Shah sitting in the next cabin. They exchanged glances from a distance. Ahmed Shah signalled that everything was okay. Bose now knew that he could get help in case he needed, so he felt more assured. This comrade left the train midway.

To his amazement, the man kept coming before him, but he never tried to come near him, he only seemed curious about, maybe he had recognised him, but he was no policeman. Bose's anxiety too had transformed into curiosity.

The journey to Peshawar was uneventful. Everything went as per the plan. The train arrived at Peshawar; here a room was already reserved for him in the Taj Mahal Hotel. As he walked out of the station with his luggage, a bag and a bedroll in hands, he found the man standing near the exit and staring at him. Only this time, he did something else besides staring at him, he bowed his eyes in a salute.

Bose had been quite flabbergasted by this man, so he thought of speaking to him. With a dash of his eyes, he asked the man to come near. He came near. Looking into his eyes, Bose asked, "Who are you?" He continued to scan him from head to toe.

"I am you," said the man in his grave voice.

"What do you mean?"

"All men belong to the same Almighty, and you are the soul of India, I am the soul too, so I am you and you are me," said the man philosophically.

"I don't have time for this philosophy. Come to the point," Bose almost chided.

"I am Subhas, it's a common name you know," said the man.

"Yes, it may be a common name, but I am Ziauddin," emphasised Bose.

"I know what you are," said the man meaningfully.

"What are you here for?" said Bose.

"To keep you free from anxiety," said the man, and while turning away, he said, "I'll be with you when you need me most."

The man walked away taking long strides, leaving behind many questions in Bose's mind. He felt somewhat assured that at least he was not a threat for him. All his journey, Bose had been thinking about this man, and finally he found that he was only a well-wisher, though his identity could not yet be clear. Before exiting out, Bose only thanked the man in his heart.

Outside the station, Bose found horse-driven tongas. On one tonga, he found one of his comrades. He headed for the second tonga, but did not know where his room was booked. He heard his comrade in the first tonga calling aloud, "Taj Mahal Hotel." It was a cue for Bose. He too asked the driver to head for the same destination.

* * * *

At Peshawar, Ahmed Shah and Bhagat Ram helped Bose. Peshawar was a border town and they had to traverse all the way to Kabul in Afghanistan on foot or horse. It was a treacherous journey indeed, as they had to pass through the Afghan post.

Physically well built, Bose looked like an Afghan, but he could not speak the Pashtun's language. Even a single word from his mouth could reveal that he was not one from the local area, and it could jeopardise his security. Bose made an effort to learn the language, but the tone and pitch could not be mastered over a period of two days; the problem was critical, but an adept solution was found out. He would act dumb, who lost his speech owing to some fever a few months ago. This excuse gave him another excuse that he was going to Afghanistan to visit the tomb at Adda Sharif to get his dumbness treated. After all, those were the ignorant times with enough room for transcendence and superstition.

The journey over the hilly, stony terrain was tough. Braving through the rocks and dust, Bose, accompanied by Bhagat Ram Talwar, trod his path on foot as well as on horse where they could find one. At some places near towns, they hitchhiked carts. They did not find much difficulty in entering Afghanistan; and this put them as good as out of the British reach, but they were not yet fully secure as the British spies were scattered around. Entering Afghanistan, Bose looked back at the vast territory he loved so dearly, and for whose freedom, he was undertaking an adventure of a lifetime. He was going away for the sake of his motherland, but he did not know whether he would be able to make it back to his place of birth. Bhagat Ram gazed at Bose whose gaze was fixed on the territory across the Afghan post that they had crossed. As Bose turned about towards his destination, his damp eyes were palpable.

"I think we should move now," said Bhagat Ram. He well knew what type of emotions rose in the mind of that patriot.

"Yes, we should," said Bose. And then he addressed his motherland with a deep voice, that seemed to echo in the mountains, "Mother, I leave you for the sake of your freedom, I'll return to get you free from the shackles of alien rule; until then I seek your forgiveness. We shall meet again. Bless me."

Bose turned towards his destination, took a few steps and then stopped again. "Now what?" Bhagat Ram was a little anxious. They had yet a long way to go.

"How do you find this place?"

"Stony and heartless, what else can you call these rocks and hills? Even plants don't grow here," said Bhagat Ram.

"No, they are so beautiful," said Bose.

"What beauty do you find here in these dry stones and pebbles?" Bhagat Ram looked at Bose as if was somewhat crazy.

"Independence…freedom…" said Bose more to himself than to Bhagat Ram.

The distance from Peshawar to Kabul was no small, it was close to 300 km, and covering this distance on foot and on horse was no child's play, especially on the stony path. It needed quite a sort of resolve, especially on part of a man who was not used to a very tough life and who had been seriously ill on more occasions than one. As an author, I would take a little liberty to explain why Bose took this route. He wanted to take the help of the Axis powers, but the British government would not have been wont to issue him a visa, especially to a country that was not on a friendly list. In these circumstances, trying to go by proper documents meant that he needed to divulge his identity, and as he was already under house arrest and surveillance of British detectives, his movement out of the country had to be kept a secret, and that is what he was trying to do. As the borders to Afghanistan were as good as unguarded, and there existed different embassies in Kabul, there were chances that he could get an asylum as well as a visa to travel to Russia or other Axis powers. He had to take such a long route and grave risk. For him, even the supreme sacrifice was not good enough if his country's freedom could not be secured. So, his route was not only stony and rocky, but also risky and perilous, it was treacherous physically as well as politically.

* * * *

Walking, riding and hitchhiking, Bose and Bhagat Ram finally made to Kabul on 27 January, 1941. They hired a room in a serai (inn).

"Tired we are," said Bhagat Ram. "What about a rest for a day!"

"Yes, tired we are," said Bose, "but not yet out. I am not here to spend time in this serai. I am out on a mission, and we must take the next step, the sooner the better."

"Yes, Comrade," said Bhagat Ram.

Bhagat Ram had connections in the Soviet embassy, but somehow they did not materialise. The Russian ambassador refused to identify Bose in his Afghan attire. The situation turned precarious, as one of the policemen already had doubted their presence. They realised that they could not hold on to the false pretensions for long. Any revelation about their identity was sure to send them back in British hands; they could not afford to do so.

"I think your efforts are not doing just fine," said Bose. "I think I should try myself."

"I am sure the things will settle down in two days, Comrade," said Bhagat Ram.

"We have been here for several days already, and I can't afford to be here any more. Come, let's go to the German embassy," said Bose.

Bose asked Bhagat Ram to engage the doorman at the embassy in talks, while Bose availed himself of the opportunity to intrude into the building.

Those were not the days of rapid news. Back home, the news about his escape had already come to light, and everybody conjectured where he could have disappeared. And when Bose suddenly burst into the German ambassador's cabin, he was reading the news story of Bose's escape.

"What brings you here? And who are you? And who allowed you to enter here?" the ambassador fired one question after another.

"I am Bose, Subhas," said Bose in a calm but confident manner.

"Are you?" the ambassador looked at the man standing before him in quite dirty Afghan attire and then at the newspaper spread before him.

"Yes, I am," said Bose taking a chair across the table.

"What a coincidence! I was reading about you," said the ambassador welcoming him. "What can I do for you?"

"I need asylum," said Bose. "I need your help to overthrow the British from India."

"I appreciate your efforts, but I can take any action only when Berlin concurs," said the ambassador.

"How long do you think it will take?"

"It must take a few days."

"Until then, you ought to give me asylum here in the embassy, my place has already been visited by the police," pleaded Bose.

"I'm sorry to say I can't do anything until I get concurrence from Berlin in the first place," said the ambassador. "And secondly, your stay in the embassy may not be secure, because several Afghans work here and we can't say it with confidence that some of them are not the British spies."

Bose had no option. He had to stay in Kabul. He now needed a safe place to stay, but it was indeed a tricky question, especially at a place where a policeman was already after him.

Bose walked out of the German embassy, yet undecided about his future course of action. He looked for Bhagat

Ram, who was standing towards the end of the street. As Bose walked, he heard a soft whisper. He turned his head. He found a man in Afghan dress trying to overtake him. As their eyes met, Bose recognised he was no other than Subhas.

"You...here?" Bose was amazed.

"There may be more avenues than you have explored. Italy is an important Axis power," said the man in a quiet whisper before gaining speed to overtake him with longer strides.

'He has a point,' Bose murmured to himself. He had never thought about Italy, whose embassy was not far away. But for now he thought it better to be with Bhagat Ram.

Bose saw Subhas once again slowing down, perhaps waiting for him to catch up. Yes, he was.

"Any thing more?" asked Bose.

"Don't place too much trust on Germany, I think Japan should be a better bet," said Subhas before once again picking up speed.

Bose nodded his head and moved on.

"We have got to wait for a few days here," said Bose to Bhagat Ram as the two began to walk side by side.

"It's a tricky question to stay in the serai," said Bhagat Ram, and then he remembered something. "I think I have a secure place where we can stay."

Bhagat Ram took Bose through several winding streets before asking him to wait in a small market. He then entered a shop. Bose could see the signboard above the shop: Master Uttamchand Crockery and Radio Store. The shopkeeper was at the counter.

"Yes, how can I serve you?" said the shopkeeper dusting his crockery in the shop.

"My salute to Comrade Uttamchand, Lal Salaam," uttered Bhagat Ram looking into his eyes. (Lal Salaam is a salutary address among the communists.)

"Do you want some money?" asked the shopkeeper in an indifferent tone.

"No, I have come here to seek a different kind of help."

"I cannot help you in any way," said Uttamchand bluntly.

"You have a golden opportunity to serve the country and party."

"Come out clean."

"I want an important revolutionary to stay in your house for a few days," said Bhagat Ram.

"I'm sorry, I can't help."

"I think you should revisit your decision."

"You are telling as if you have brought Bose. I'm sorry."

"Yes."

"What yes?"

"Yes, Bose is right here with me. I want refuge for him, but any way, you're not willing to help," said Bhagat Ram in a firm voice. "I'll manage elsewhere."

Saying these words, Bhagat Ram quickly climbed down the stairs and scarce he had taken a couple of steps than Uttamchand rushed to the door and called him from behind.

"You are welcome," he said.

Uttamchand was an old revolutionary and communist from the Punjab, who had been to jail on charges related to work against the government, who got out of the country to avoid trouble under the family's pressure, and was now running this shop in Kabul. But the very idea of coming in proximity of Bose had shaken awake his patriotism; he was once again ready to risk himself for the sake of one of the greatest leaders, whose work promised freedom for the country.

Uttamchand welcomed Bose into the house, but his wife did not display a matching enthusiasm, chiefly because of their attire, as both Bose and Bhagat Ram were camouflaged as Afghans. She was reluctant even to give them food, let alone allow them to stay in the house. He was pressurised into revealing their identity, on the oath of keeping it a secret, and this changed her demeanour. She served her guests in a spirit that Punjabi Khatris are known for. Bose too felt grateful, especially for the homemade food that he was looking for, and it tasted still better when it was wrapped in affectionate sentiments.

Settled in the house, Bose recalled Subhas's words regarding Italy. Next day, he sent Bhagat Ram to explore chances with the Italian embassies, and he was greatly relieved that they had already been contacted by Germany and they together were willing to help him out. But getting papers made needed time, as means of transport and communication were not as swift as they are now. Bose's photograph was sent to Rome, and a few days later, his passport was ready in the name of Count Orlando Mazzotta. May we tell you that 'Count' is a rank from nobility, and it shows the importance that the Axis powers attached to him.

It was after two months from the time of his flight from his house arrest, precisely on 18 March, 1941, when Bose crossed over to the Russian territory on an Italian transit visa. He had with him an Italian and two German assistants. Before leaving, Bose bid sentimental adieu to Bhagat Ram who had taken great pains for his cause. There was no way he could take Bhagat Ram with him, though he wanted to. The wife of Uttamchand displayed her patriotic spirits when she handed over three gold coins which she had inherited from her mother. Bose left with sweet memories of Kabul, but he had no time to think about them, as he had before him great goals to be accomplished.

'Maybe I'll get time to think about all these small but important events of my life,' murmured Bose to himself while travelling into Russian territory.

* * * *

Bose headed for Moscow at first. He explored any possibilities of getting assistance in his national cause, but found the response disappointing. The Soviets were more interested in the Balkans than Asian territories beyond troublesome Afghanistan. So, for Bose, his main destination became Berlin, he now pinned all his hopes on Germany, he flew to Berlin on 28 March, 1941, by a special chartered plane. He landed in Berlin finally on 3 April, 1941. He was making all possible efforts towards realisation of his goal, leaving behind his marks on the sand of time.

Back home, the British government was bewildered where Bose had gone. His family members made out that he had possibly become a monk and had left for Pondicherry. The government had no clue, but soon it was going to know about his escapade.

* * * *

Bose had pinned his hopes on Germany for two reasons. It had entered the treaty of non-aggression with Soviet Russia; and secondly, there were a sizeable number of Indian soldiers, who had been taken prisoner by General Rommel during his operations in Africa. Bose intended to recruit these soldiers into an expeditionary army and with Germany's help, march them through Russia and Afghanistan to attack on northwestern India. He was confident that as soon as he did this, all Indians would rise in revolt against the British, who were already trapped in the global war, and it would become impossible for them to deal with the revolution at such a massive scale.

Bose had done his homework well. He had gathered all statistics which he could use to convince the German leadership; it provided force to what he wanted to convince the German establishment. India, as a British colony, had contributed to the British war effort tremendously, with both men and materials. The Indian soldiers had proved their mettle in different wars that the British had fought right since their occupation of India in 1757; it was mainly on the strength of the Indians that the British had succeeded to subjugate India. And without doubt, it were the very Indian soldiers who had risen in revolt several times, the most catastrophic being in 1857, which shook the foundation of the British East India Company's rule in India, and resulting into the British Crown taking over the administration. The Indians had shown their war skills in numerous battles fought on land, in air and on water. The Indian Air Force was in its nascent stages, but whatever responsibility it was being assigned, it was leaving behind a mark, forcing the British masters to finalise upon its expansion. It was on the Indians' strength that the British had won many battles during the First World War; and they were achieving this feat again during the Second World War. General Rommel himself had admired the Indian soldiers in Africa.

It was true, as Bose noted in his letter to the German authorities, that the defeat of the British was a necessary corollary to India's independence, and this defeat hinged upon cutting off the Indian supplies of men and materials to the British. The things, however, were not as rosy as they seemed to be. They had their negative aspects too.

All of Germany, Italy and Japan, the three main factors of the Axis alliance, had imperialistic tendencies, no different than those of Britain and France, rather worse than them. Russia, presently neutral, too had imperialistic tendencies, which it was displaying in Poland and other Balkan states. If India won its freedom with the help of German and Russian forces, it would be next to impossible to convince them to leave. This could simply lead India from a bad to worse situation, and you could not trust them. It was Bose's predicament, nevertheless he was confident that he could thwart any such move on part of these Axis powers.

Once in Berlin, Bose was confident that he would be able to win the support of the Germans. Deep in his heart, he was a little scared too if he would come across disappointing attitude from Germany too, because it was already on the course of expanding its war zones in the western Europe and its relations with Russia were no more as cordial as they were at the start of the world war. Bose's seeking the Russian help could not be successful because of several reasons, an important factor being the manpower. On the other hand, there were almost 4,500 Indian soldiers held as prisoners of war in Germany, and an expeditionary army could be created with them. This would only relieve Germany of their responsibility of looking after them. This strength was not enough, but Bose hoped that he would convince the Indian immigrants in Germany to join hands with him.

The first thing that Bose did on reaching the German soil was to write a secret letter to the German government. He started it with a mention of the British policies that hinged on malicious intent towards the Indians. He mentioned in it that despite its assurance during the First World War, Britain had not relaxed its hold on India, and in the present war, it was heavily relying on Indian resources. So, India wished to see Britain to be defeated soundly in this war so that its aspiration of independence could be brought into reality. He stressed that Indians were fully disenchanted with the British, and it was the most opportune time when the British could be rooted out of India.

Bose further stated that India and the Axis alliance would come together to form a grand alliance with India and Afghanistan as members. A government of free India in exile would be set up in Germany and an Azad Hind Radio would be set up which would broadcast necessary programmes to boost revolution in India. The outcome would be the victory of the Axis powers, and it would further culminate into a treaty between India and other Axis powers, which would help India to stand on its feet economically and politically, while India, on its part, would do everything to repay this debt.

This letter, however, remained unanswered.

A week later, Bose wrote another letter to the German government. It mainly contained five points, including a request for declaration of independence for India and other British colonies, inciting revolt in these countries, invasion of Britain by Axis powers in order to divide the British attention, and assistance for Iraq, if needed, for war against Britain. He concluded his letter saying that these steps would create a long chain of friendly nations, right from northern

Africa to the Far East and Japan; and in case, it became inevitable for Germany to come into conflict with Turkey or Russia, it would be in an advantageous position.

This trick proved its worth. Germany was aware of the status and popularity Bose enjoyed in India, which was at par with that of Gandhiji, in some respects, even more than him. Given a chance, Bose was capable of starting a massive revolution and was capable of shaking the very foundation of the British Empire; this simply meant a rather comfortable victory over Britain, which was already at the receiving end in the Second World War. A victory over Britain simply meant Axis victory in the Second World War.

However, Germany still nursed several types of apprehensions, so the foreign office got in touch with Bose. The most pertinent question that perturbed the Germans was that the Indian leadership in India was not well disposed towards Germany, especially Hitler. He was explained that in this land of the Nazis, nothing could move without the consent of Adolf Hitler.

Bose explained, "There are reasons if the Indian leadership is not so well disposed towards Germany. In his autobiography, the Führer has said that Britain had civilised India, though the fact is that Indian civilisation goes back to over five thousand years, while the European civilisation is of later origin. This mindset needs to be amended on part of Germany."

Germany was also of the view that there would be chaos in India if Britain were to leave India all of a sudden.

Bose was quite clear on this point. He said, "A national government will be formed."

The foreign officer interrupted, "You mean you as the head of the nation?"

"No," said Bose emphatically. "It will be a democratically elected government by the people."

Yet another pertinent query from Germany was about the existence of a number of communities in India, and there would be animosity between them, especially between the two major communities – Hindus and Muslims. At this point of time, incidences of communal riots were being reported in the international media.

Bose had a satisfactory explanation to this point as well. He said, "Well, we have several communities, but we have been this way for centuries. A massive country like India is bound to have a few differences of opinion, but that never means we cannot solve them ourselves."

The German foreign office was quite convinced about these queries, but it had more serious questions to ask, and Bose embraced the opportunity well. The main query remained how it could be possible for Indians to drive out the British, because it was a powerful empire with a strong army and massive resources.

Bose said, "Well, you see the might of the British in India is fully dependent on the Indians. The British government has only 70,000 British soldiers and officers, and the rest of its army is constituted of Indians. In the ongoing world war even, a large portion of British forces is formed by the Indians who are contributing to the British operations significantly; they have made their presence felt on all fronts they are fighting. When the Indian National Army marches into India, all Indians would switch sides, not only this, masses would rise in support of independence from the atrocious British. In such a case, it would not be possible for these handfuls of British soldiers and officers to continue to hold on to India. They will have to leave Indian territory sooner than later."

And now the most pertinent query came up. The foreign secretary asked, "How strong an army will you need then?"

"A 50,000-men strong army will be enough," said Bose.

"But where from will these 50,000 men come?"

Bose had done his homework well. He said with a smile on his lips, "From the POWs that you have with you, and from those who have been captured by Japan and Italy. I also hope that the Indians living in other countries too would join."

"Well, we wish good luck to you and the Indians," said the foreign secretary.

The German establishment got in touch with Italy on this point, and the two agreed to Bose's points in principle.

* * * *

Bose soon found trusted Indians in Germany who could assist in his mission. Two notable comrades included A.C.N.

Nambiar, a journalist, and Ganpule, a former member of the Bombay Congress. Abid Hasan, a former Congress activist, too was in Germany at this time, and he joined as Bose's secretary. The Indian POWs (prisoners of war) in Berlin were not so enthusiastic about joining Bose's cause, as they felt confused whether they should stick to the oath of allegiance to the British they had taken at the time of their recruitment, or switch their loyalty. They had to be convinced about the noble cause of the motherland's freedom. Of the total of 4,500 POWs, about 3,000 came over, and this was how the Free India Legion or Azad Hind Fauz was formed. Its strength grew to about 4,500 in a couple of months. Germany also agreed to equip them with military equipment as well as train them in modern warfare.

Germany agreed to give economic aid and set up a radio station. All these functioned under the direct control of the Free India Centre, with its headquarters in Berlin under the direct command of Bose. Overall administrative control was under the German secret service, Waffen-SS.

The Indian Legion was formed on 2 October, 1941, the birthday of Mahatma Gandhi. Bose invited the Indian immigrants in the ceremony. The new oath was taken by the soldiers accepting Adolf Hitler and Subhas as the leaders. Expressing loyalty to Adolf Hitler was born out of the necessity as without his cooperation, India's cause could not have been furthered.

Availing this opportunity, Bose addressed those present there. He expressed hope that his mission would culminate into freedom for the motherland. He made people to vow that they would be ready to sacrifice everything for the sake of their country. He also gave the slogan of 'Jai Hind' to the Free India Legion, which has stood the test of times; even today, it echoes in the Indians' hearts, it is called in any meeting or assembly of political significance; and for many, it has become a salutary term, especially among children and soldiers.

The Free India Centre was established with only 35 comrades, mainly students, but as they worked, it started to expand rapidly. The first meeting of this newly established organisation was held a month later on 2 November.

Now, Bose emerged as a popular leader of international stature. The Jana-Gana-Mana, a poem by Rabindranath Tagore, was accepted as the national anthem. After independence, this poem has been approved as India's national anthem with some deviation.

Looking at India's diversity, Bose favoured a mixture of languages as a common link among the people of India, he termed it Hindustani, which was mainly a blend of Hindi and Urdu, and he recommended to adopt the Roman script as the national script.

The flag of the government of Free India in exile was the Tricolour, with a leaping lion in the middle; and words 'Azad' on the top stripe and 'Hind' on the lower stripe; this pattern had been drawn by Bose himself.

With all these provisions, the Free India Centre started to function. A team of ten people was formed to look after the work of the Azad Hind Radio, which was assigned to broadcast a 45-minute programme daily. This team was assigned to collect, edit and translate different news reports and other materials. Broadcast on short-wave, this radio was gradually becoming popular with the Indian masses back home. The idea behind setting up the radio service was to provide the Indians a source of reliable information, because the British radio often indulged in propaganda, and the Indians were being deprived of objective reports from the battlefield as well as from political front. This radio was also to prove an instrument in motivating Indians to participate in the national cause. It was a sort of great achievement for Bose when he made the Germans agree that the Azad Hind Radio would function as an autonomous institution, and its programmes would not be censored. It was to be a sort of secret service operating from a secret location.

The British had prohibited all kinds of propaganda in India, but they never knew how to deal with the Azad Hind Radio; it chose to start a frequency very close to the short-wave transmission so that people would not be able to listen to it very clearly, but people did, they waited for its programmes eagerly which became a point of discussion.

* * * *

All these achievements might seem quite attractive, but so was not the case in fact. The first great jolt to Bose's efforts came on 22 June, 1941, when Germany decided to roll its tanks into Russia. After the fall of France, Hitler thought that defeating England was no big game, so he started to shift his land forces from western sector to eastern sector, thinking that England could be well dealt by its air force. It was to be one of the gravest strategic errors on part of Hitler. Despite bombing England, particularly London, day and night, he could not break the will of the English people; the more he bombed, the more motivated they became. Hitler had tried to create one more enemy before having annihilated the previous one. His sense of urgency could be understood by the fact that the situation in snow-bound Russia becomes very unfavourable in winters, and Hitler wanted to finish occupation of the Russian territory before the onset of winters, but he had underestimated the challenge. In this bid, he had left alone England, which had all the potential to reverse the German gains.

Bose was devastated from this action. After initial successes, Germany had started to commit grave mistakes in the war. It dumped the non-aggression pact and attacked the Soviet Union thinking that it would fall within eight weeks. Adolf Hitler grossly underestimated the strength of the Russians; he thought that Russia would be brought to heels before the winters began. It brought about opening up of a long frontier at war. Also, Britain and the United States of America aided the Soviet Union in its fight against Germany, thus giving rise to their unity, which ultimately proved the death knell for the Axis powers.

This gross error on part of Adolf Hitler had also risked the very aspiration of Bose, whose plan needed the cooperation of Germany and Russia to succeed, but these new uncalled-for hostilities had all the seeds of thwarting his plan of invading northwestern India through Russia and Afghanistan.

It was time for Bose to introspect. The most potent question before him was – Will he fail in his mission? The German attack on Russia could possibly result into it. He was dejected and disappointed to some degree. Putting off lights, he sat on the floor. He wanted to meditate. In the past few years, he had not been able to meditate properly. Meditation gave him strength of the mind, and he needed it all the more in view of the new developments.

He closed his eyes, and the first thing to do was complain to God, "I propose, and you dispose." He wondered what the future had in store for him and India.

Bose had contested election for the post of the Congress President and won it in 1938, but he was forced out of it by Mahatma Gandhi. Had he been the President, he would not need to escape and come all the way to the foreign soil seeking help from the powers he little trusted. He had massive plans to launch the Civil Disobedience Movement to shake the British foundations. But politics prevailed over his good intentions. If people went for selfish interests, India would not be able to win an all-encompassing victory, it would not get victory that would be complete in all respects. He was perturbed that despite the most opportune moment for launching the national movement for freedom of the country, the Congress was doing nothing. The British government would have been the most susceptible to pressure at this point of time, but Gandhiji did not wish to pressurise it. 'How can we cope with an enemy who is unwilling to see our point of view?' murmured Bose, but out of anguish, his voice seemed to echo in the room. He tried to concentrate his thoughts. He had to chalk out his future programmes and plans carefully. In any case, he did not want the opportunity to slip out of his hands.

Bose had chosen the unsavoury Germany, because he thought that it needed 'a poison to kill a poison'. But now, once again, his plan to invade India had been rendered impracticable with Hitler rolling his tanks into Russia. Invasion of northwestern India through Russia and Afghanistan was no longer possible. Germany was confident that it would earn victory before the winters started, but this could not be possible, Bose knew. The Russians were nationalists, they would leave no stone unturned to throw the Germans out of their land. The conflict was sure to last much longer, right until the world war lasted, but Bose did not have that much of time. He had to think of the alternatives. He remembered what Subhas had once advised him in Afghanistan. Bose now decided to explore avenues with Japan.

Bose was completely at the mercy of Adolf Hitler, and when the German forces started to meet one reverse after another on the Soviet front, he became restless. He needed to review his entire plan. He had no hope of his plan being successful, especially in view of stiff resistance by the

Russians. He knew it well that the onset of winters would only mean total annihilation of the German forces in Russia as the supply lines would be too long to maintain and reinforce. How the Russians confronted the Germans and turned scales is a heroic tale of the Second World War.

After initial successes in Russia, Germany was now facing grave challenges. At several places, it had to retreat. It simply meant that Germany would no more be in a position of rendering any help to Bose to drive the British out of India. Its assistance in maintaining the Indian Legion seemed more of a political propaganda rather than a military strategy.

Bose was yet to comprehend the gravity of these new developments when he was faced with yet another trauma – the entry of the U.S. in the war. Until the end of 1941, America was more interested in contributing in the war through supply of arms and equipment. It was a turning point in the global war in favour of the Allied forces.

Maintaining complete radio silence, the Japanese naval fleet sailed all the way from Japan to Hawaii and launch a surprise attack on Pearl Harbor with a devastating result. Almost the entire Pacific Fleet of America was destroyed with a loss of 20 ships, 250 aircraft, and 3,000 men among other losses. This attack occurred on the small hours of 7 December, 1941, and took America by surprise. No one had ever imagined that Japan could go to this extent. Ironically, some early warning had been there, but no one bothered to check it, because no one simply believed that Pearl Harbor could be accessed by any enemy ships. America was stunned by this attack, and it decided to enter the world war.

If you wanted to know the two gravest errors on part of the Axis powers, these were German invasion of Soviet Russia and Japan's attack on Pearl Harbor, both of which had the potential of not only thwarting the strategic schemes of the Axis powers, but also bringing them to their knees in the times to come.

These two errors came like a blessing in disguise for the Allied forces, but not for Bose. His hopes hinged on Axis powers. He was greatly perturbed, but he started to see a ray of hope from another front. It was Japanese success in Asia and the Pacific despite America's entry in the war. He had seen his chances of invading India from the northeast, bordering Burma, where Japan was pitched well and advancing ahead. But it was no easy for him to shift from Germany to Japan.

* * * *

The news of Japanese success in the Pacific was quite encouraging for Bose. When Japan defeated Britain and occupied Singapore, Bose thought that it was an occasion to celebrate. He decided to address the masses on radio himself. It was his first address which happened on 19 February, 1942. It was his first communication with his countrymen after his escape from the house arrest the previous year.

In his address, Bose said: "I have been waiting silently and patiently for the events to unfold in our favour, and now, when the events have started to occur in our favour, it is the most opportune time I should speak to you. Pitching myself high on the historical achievements, I, on behalf of all freedom-loving Indian migrants, declare that we will continue to struggle against British imperialism continuously until we become the makers of our fortune ourselves. During the course of our national movement for freedom and later during the course of reconstruction of our motherland, we are intent upon cooperating with those who will assist us in uprooting the enemy from our native land.

The fall of Britain in Singapore is the beginning of the complete fall of the British empire from the world. It is a new dawn on the horizon. Shackled in the chains of slavery, we have lost our sense of morality and economics; but now the Almighty has presented to us an auspicious occasion to liberate India. In this age, there is no greater enemy of freedom and progress than Britain. After my escape from India, the British government has been giving you false contradictory reports. In these calamitous times, the British government would have been elated beyond limits to see me dead, but the Supreme Entity has something else in store.

Friends, there is no need for my countrymen to bow before any Englishman, because we carry on our shoulders the pride and glory of India. I earnestly hope that you will unite and cooperate in the struggle that I have launched. We can together destroy the British Empire. I entreat all Indians to bind themselves together and jump into the struggle for freedom.

Jai Hind!"

In India, the Indians had abandoned all their hopes about Bose being alive. Their joy knew no bounds when they came to know that the leader, they loved so ardently, not only was alive, but also was making great efforts for freedom of the country. But this news was not so delightful for the British. Already constrained in the world war, this news had all the chances of creating turmoil and disturbance in India, which it was sure to find difficult to deal with. Bose's joining hands with its enemies had created a great upheaval in England. The Indians had received a piece of good news after a long time.

* * * *

As of May, Germany had not acceded to Bose's demand of declaring the government of free India in exile, let alone its future post-war policy so far as freedom of India was concerned. Bose was already thinking about his future course of action, when he found that both Japan and Italy had agreed to India's freedom, but Germany was yet to say a word about it. It was difficult for him to continue with this kind of uncertainty. So, he decided to meet Adolf Hitler. It was after untiring efforts on part of Bose that Hitler, the most dangerous personality of the world, agreed to meet him.

Bose had several points of disagreement with Hitler, especially his remark in his autobiography *Mein Kampf*, which said that Indians' effort for freedom had no chance of success until Britain was defeated by a more powerful military power. He further wrote that it would be better to see it continue under British subjugation than to assist an uncivilized and uncontrollable India.

Hitler, on the other hand, had reservations about Indian leaders, especially those of the Congress, who did not hold a sympathetic view of the German aggressive policies. An acute problem with Hitler's mindset was that he considered the Germans as racially superior to the dark-skinned people, and Indians were no exception. To bring him to the favourable side, it was necessary that this kind of thinking was overcome.

Right in the beginning of the meeting, Bose raised his remark that he had made in his autobiography, but Hitler refused to comment. Coming to the main point of his agenda, Bose asked, "Will the German government declare about India's independence after the war?"

Hitler thought for a while and then said in his trade-mark style, "India won't be capable to rule itself for another one century and a half."

It was too rude for Bose to digest. His patience was giving way, but he somehow controlled himself in order to know what resided in Hitler's mind. He asked about German plans to invade India. Hitler bluntly said that India was far off from the German fronts, and there could not emanate any practical benefit from declaring India's freedom at that juncture.

Bose was stunned. It meant that Germany had no plans for India's freedom. The chance of its direct assistance in India's struggle for freedom was like a pipe dream. Moreover, it appeared that even with the remote chances of Germany driving out the British, it would be unwilling to vacate India. Actually, Bose had been much uncomfortable about this point, and it was coming out in the open. He could no more trust Germany.

Bose was trying to come to terms with his disappointment when Hitler asked him, "When circumstances are so adverse, what steps would you take for India's freedom movement?"

By this time, Bose was impatient too. He said to the interpreter standing by, "Tell him that I have lived all my life in politics, and I don't need anyone's concurrence in this regard."

The meeting had ended in a failure and disillusionment for Bose, but Hitler was profoundly impressed by Bose's personality and ideology. It was owing to this impression that Hitler later removed the objectionable remark about India from his autobiography. It could be described no trivial achievement looking at Hitler's stubbornness. Another positive aspect for Bose was that Hitler agreed to transport him to Japan. Towards the end of the meeting, Hitler remarked that Japan could be more useful to Bose as it was fighting in Southeast Asia, quite close to India's northeastern borders.

It was what Bose had already been thinking. He said, "It would be a great help for me if you can arrange an aircraft for me to fly to Japan."

Hitler's reply to this request was quite assuaging his feelings. He said, "Bose, do you want to travel half the globe in an aeroplane, especially during the ongoing hostilities? No, I can't take that risk. Rather I'll send you by the sea. My U-boat will carry you all the way to Japan."

Bose shook hands with Hitler and walked out of the cabin with mixed feelings. This meeting took place on 29 May, 1942.

* * * *

Bose had decided to move from Germany to Japan, but it could not be done without leaving behind repercussions in Germany. It was sure that Germany would not agree to transport his men of the Indian Legion to Asia; this meant that they would have to be abandoned. It was a very disturbing thought. Days after days were passing in a hurry, and there was no hope in sight for Bose to move from Germany to Asia for which Hitler himself had assured help. It entailed that there could be little hope for the large number of soldiers to go to the war theatre.

Bose was worried that these soldiers could be sent to another front by Germany; he never wanted his men to become cannon fodder for the Germans, but there was little he could do.

Bose got in touch with the Japanese embassy in Berlin. And he had a piece of encouraging news in store for him. The Azad Hind Fauz or Indian National Army (INA) was being formed in Singapore with the Indian expatriates and prisoners of war. It was a piece of great news; he was now curious to reach where the action for national freedom could be taken.

* * * *

How did Bose get an idea about forming an Indian Legion that could incite the Indian troops in the Royal British Indian Army for a revolt? I think it would be better to look in the past times for a better understanding.

Swami Vivekananda died in the prime of his youth in 1902, but not before lighting a flame of nationalism among the Indians. He awakened India spiritually as well as infused in masses a sense of patriotism.

At the start of the twentieth century, people were becoming gradually disillusioned with the Congress's moderate policies towards the British. They had seen the indifferent attitude of the British towards the famine in 1896-97 and plague in 1899-1901. Even leaders in the Congress were becoming impatient towards the petitions being filed by the Congress to the British government, which was more than inclined to reject them as it took them very lightly. When petitions by the moderate leaders brought no change in the British attitude, the young Indians grew restless and felt that no purpose could be served without active struggle. The British were mercilessly exploiting the Indians economically. The Congress activities led to spreading awareness about the national cause; social and religious awakening too contributed in this. They lost faith in the peaceful constitutional process and came to believe that they needed to be out in the streets to directly come into conflict with the British power. This led to the rise of extremists within the Congress and revolutionaries outside it. These sentiments gained further fillip due to the Delhi Darbar in 1903 and partition of Bengal in 1905. While the Delhi Darbar had been organised overlooking the plight of the Indians' suffering in numerous ways; the partition of Bengal was aimed at dividing the Hindu and Muslim communities along religious lines with a view to sow eternal animosity between them, though on the face of it, they cited the reason for partition of the province of Bengal as it was too large to govern. The Indians had seen through this intent and the mischief that Lord Curzon had made, and they rose in protest. They opposed the partition tooth and nail. A long struggle followed and the British were compelled to repeal the partition in 1911. This was a sort of victory for the extremist faction within the Congress, and now people believed that they could confront the British successfully.

Let us distinguish between the extremist Congress leaders and the revolutionaries. The extremist leaders did not believe in violence. They adopted such means as protests, processions, criticism, boycott of foreign goods, picketing of liquor and foreign goods shops, using Swadeshi. They also helped espouse the cause of self-reliance, self-confidence and self-respect in the Indians. They did not want the government's mercy, they wanted their demands to be fulfilled as their basic rights. While the petitioners were satisfied with limited self-government under the British government, the extremists went ahead to demand outright freedom. Bal Gangadhar Tilak set the path when he roared, "Swaraj is my birthright and I shall have it." They were gravely appalled when the Congress chose to support Britain in their war effort in the First World War. A little prior to the start of the first great war, Britain was sceptical that the people of India and Indian leadership could avail this opportunity to rise in a rebellion; it would have pressurised Britain greatly. On the contrary, the Indians were ever more willing to help Britain in the war with both men and materials. The success of the Allied forces in the First World War was quite contributed with human and material resources from India.

The Congress leadership was optimistic that its support to Britain during the war would lead to favourable outcomes for it as well as the country. When the revolutionaries saw that the Congress was little bothered about independence and was satisfied with small favours, they wished to drive the British out of the country. They were convinced that this could not be done without an armed rebellion, but how could they do it? This came in the form of revolutionary activities within the country and Ghadar Party.

The Ghadar Party, initially the Pacific Coast Hindustan Association, was formed in 1913 by the revolutionaries in the U.S. and Canada like Lala Har Dayal, Bhai Parmanand, Mohammad Barakatullah, and Sohan Singh Bhakna among others. These leaders planned to raise an armed rebellion, collect money and resources, buy guns and ammunition, and motivate the Indian troops in the Royal British Indian

Army to rise in revolt. It gained support from the Indian expatriates and also contacted several units in the Punjab and Bengal provinces. It also gained substantive funding from the German government. The party had active members in several countries including Mexico, Japan, China, Singapore, Thailand, Philippines, Malaya, Indo-China and Eastern and Southern Africa. This clearly shows the impact the party was having in the world, and why the British were scared of it.

The Ghadar Party was operating with the basic idea that most of the military troops of the Royal British Indian Army were deployed out of India, and there were only a small number of them left back in India, who could be motivated to join them in the rebellion. The party was becoming popular during the First World War, and an effort was being made to realise its goal of armed rebellion in India by Indian troops, when the Komagata Maru incident happened in 1914. Owing to the British exploitation, the people in Punjab were in a bad condition economically and they were looking for better avenues elsewhere, and seeing opportunities in Canada, they went there in large numbers. However, Britain did not want a large number of Indians there. In order to limit the number of Indian immigrants to Canada, then a colony of Britain, an anti-Indian immigration law was passed, by which strict conditions were enforced so that the Indians could not get entry in Canada. The main clause was the condition of 'continuous journey regulation', which was enacted only to restrict ships direct from India. The distance from India to Canada being very long, the ships were bound, in those days, to have at least a stop over in Japan or China, but Gurdit Singh decided to think of circumventing this regulation. He hired the ship called Komagata Maru in Hong Kong and sailed all the way to Vancouver; still the Canadian authorities were not interested because all passengers in it were Indians. Of the 376 passengers from India, chiefly Punjab, only 24 were allowed entry, and the rest were forced to go back to India. When the ship arrived at Budge Budge, near Calcutta (now Kolkata), the passengers were harassed, leading to a conflict, in which 19 passengers were killed. Some escaped, but most of them were imprisoned; some of them were also put under village arrest during the First World War. The plight of the passengers of the ship can be gauged from the fact that the ship set sail from Hong Kong on 4 April, and stopped at Shanghai, China and Yokohama, Japan and reached Vancouver on 23 May, and set sail back to India on 23 July, and during its stay at the harbour, the passengers were not allowed to disembark, leave alone immigrate; this shows the barbaric attitude of the authorities. The ship reached back Calcutta on 27 September. Just imagine the kind of pitiable, deplorable condition the passengers must have faced during their stay aboard the ship for over five months and a half, especially in the days when the ships were not equipped with facilities as they are now. And also imagine the 'welcome' they received at Calcutta: they had to face the firing squad.

Whatever the plight of the passengers on the Komagata Maru, it served well to give prominence to the cause of the Ghadar Party. It sent a large number of volunteers to India in 1915; however, the British government came to know of the plan, and foiled the attempt. The British government sentenced a large number of these revolutionaries to death and incarcerated many to life sentence in Kala Pani or Andaman. The final sentence, delivered under the Defence of India Act of 1915, gave death sentence to 42, life sentence to 114, and 93 were sent for varying terms of imprisonment. This case is better known as Lahore Conspiracy Case.

Rash Behari Bose was one of the leaders of the Ghadar Party, who escaped from Lahore in India to Japan in May 1915. The British tried its best with the Japanese authorities for his extradition, but to no avail. Later, he married a Japanese citizen and became a Japanese citizen by naturalisation. However, his interest in India's independence continued, and this was why he set up the Indian Independence League.

The effort by other Indians abroad too had brought the issue of India's independence to prominence at the international level. Revolutionary activities were being planned and encouraged by the India House, set up by Shyamji Krishna Varma, in London. This organisation had profound effect on shaping revolutionary ideas on Indian students abroad. Many eminent Indians came into contact with such revolutionary entities. They published newspapers and pamphlets to espouse the Indian cause. The list of these revolutionaries is very long, they helped to liberate India from the British clutches and had profound impact on the Indians, both at home and abroad.

* * * *

While Bose waited for his journey from Berlin to Japan, he continued to ponder over the outcome of the First World War and its repercussions on India.

'Why doesn't the Congress learn a lesson from the past experience?' murmured the anguished Bose sitting in his room alone.

During the course of the First World War, the British government wanted to concentrate on the war, so it wanted to be relieved of the anxiety that the extremists and revolutionaries were creating. The extremist leaders of the Congress, led by Bal Gangadhar Tilak and Annie Besant, were becoming vocal and now demanding self-government for India. This movement is better called the Indian Home Rule Movement. This demand grew in popularity, and pressurised the Congress too to embrace it as its aim.

In order to pacify the Indian national movement and pacify the Indians' belligerent sentiments, the British government, in 1917, declared that it would increase association of Indians in every branch of administration and self-governing institutions would be introduced gradually. However, at the end of the war in 1918, the Government of India Act, 1919, was passed, popularly called Montague-Chelmsford Reforms. Belying the Indians' trust, it provided for separate or communal electorates. The war had had terrible impact on the Indians' economy; they were reeling under the extreme pressure, and when they wanted to raise their voice against this law, the Rowlatt Act, 1919, was rather introduced. This act empowered the police to imprison any person without trial and conviction for as long as two years.

In protest against this act, the National Humiliation Day was observed on 6 April, 1919, all over India. Punjab was no exception. It had been a hotbed of revolutionary and nationalist activities. When two of its popular leaders, Satyapal and Dr. Saifuddin Kitchlew were arrested on 10 April, people decided to hold a protest on 13 April at Jallianwala Bagh in Amritsar. It was also the day of Baisakhi, a popular Punjabi festival.

The crowd that gathered for a peaceful protest in the Bagh also had women and children in large numbers. This Bagh is surrounded by high walls on three sides with a narrow entry on one side. General Dyer, the military commander of Amritsar, came with his troops and occupied the only entrance. He then ordered his troops to fire at the crowd without any warning. When some troops fired in the air, he specifically ordered them to fire at people and kill them. The hopeless people had nowhere to escape. Many of them jumped into the dry wells on one side of the park; the people to jump first were crushed under the weight of the people who jumped in later. Many tried to escape by climbing over the walls, but this made them prominent targets of the firing squad. The troops went on firing until the last bullet, only then General Dyer left the scene. He left behind him a terrible situation, with piles of dead bodies and groans of the injured men, women and children, with no respite or medical aid.

According to the Congress, more than 1,000 people were killed, while another 2,000 were wounded, though the government put the number of casualties at less than 400. The British government proclaimed the Martial Law and continued with its repressive measures, but it only made the revolutionaries more determined and resolved to fight back.

'When the Congress has seen the outcome of the First World War being so terrible for Indians, why doesn't it start agitation against the foreign government?' asked Bose, but had no one to answer to him.

* * * *

The Indian Independence League too had a role in organising nationalist movement in Southeast Asia, especially bolstered by the Japanese after it occupied Malaya. A framework of the league in the form of several different organisations of Indians existed in the Southeast before Japan came to occupy it. With the Japanese encouragement, all these organisations came together to form the Indian Independence League (IIL), and it was the main instrument of the local Indian population interacting with the Japanese occupation force. The Japanese encouragement came in various forms; for example, it brought the members security and perks, who were issued IIL cards, which helped them buy railway tickets and other hard-to-get items like rations, toothpaste and soap at reasonable prices. It also helped them send letters to other countries. When Rash Behari Bose fled to Japan, he contributed in shaping, expanding and amalgamating the Indian freedom movement.

However, many leaders were wary of Japan's vested interests as it was an occupying force in this part of the world, and this was the reason that the Tokyo Conference, held in March 1942, failed. However, most Indians living there supported it, especially when it took measures to improve the lot of the Indian plantation labourers. It was in the Bangkok Conference, held in June 1942, that the Indian Independence League came into being officially. It had two departments: a Council for Action and a Committee of Representatives. Rash Behari Bose was the chairman of the council. Under it, Mohan Singh was one of the members who had founded the Indian National Army (INA) from the prisoners of war whom Japan had captured; and thus, the INA was made subordinate to the Council.

So far as the League's relationship with Japan was concerned, it demanded assurance for respect for India's sovereignty and territorial integrity, and sought further cooperation for independence. One of its main demands was to accord the Indian National Army the status of an allied army and its strength should be raised by releasing all Indian POWs to it. It also demanded of Japan to equip and train the INA troops and officers.

* * * *

The Indian National Army had been formed in 1942, much before Bose's arrival in Southeast Asia. After the fall of Singapore, the INA was raised by Mohan Singh with the support of Japan. Mohan Singh was a captain with the British army, who had seen action against the Japanese forces in the battle of Jitra, where his troops were outgunned and captured. He was taken to Major Fujiwara, the main Japanese officer who encouraged formation of the Indian National Army. It was Fujiwara who convinced Mohan Singh to form the force with the broader purpose of India's independence. He also promised that Mohan Singh and his troops would be treated as allies and friends, and not as POWs.

The INA mainly consisted of 12,000 Indian troops of the total 40,000 Indian POWs, who were taken prisoner during the Malayan campaign or who had surrendered at Singapore. It was formally proclaimed in June 1942, but a sense of distrust prevailed among the constituents, especially with regard to the Japanese intentions. As it was made subordinate to the Indian Independence League, the Indian troops thought that Rash Behari Bose, now a naturalised Japanese, had his vested interests to serve. Ultimately, the INA was dissolved in December 1942.

However, when Bose arrived in the region, it was revived, and most of the initial volunteers in it joined the INA for its final action for freedom.

A moot point is: Why did the Indians distrust the Japanese and German intentions? Japan is a Buddhist nation, and it looks to India for inspiration and spiritualism; so it enjoyed a high ground, especially in view of the progress it made in industrialisation. Its status was further exalted among Indians after its victory over Russia in 1905. However, when it started invasion of China, the Indians were sceptical about its intentions that it could replace Britain as the masters of India; that simply meant that one imperialistic power was replaced with another, and it was seen even more ruthless and cruel than Britain. In Singapore too, the Japanese spared Indian POWs and expatriates, but cruelly massacred the Chinese and other European people, instilling fear of the cruel nature of Japanese imperialism. It was the precise reason that the Indians did not take kindly to the Japanese effort to raise an army from the Indian troops and expatriates.

With the passage of time towards the close of 1942, the Indian troops and officers began to increasingly feel that they were mere pawns in the hands of the Japanese, as their operations were being interfered into by them. The Japanese also tried to censor Indian broadcasts in Singapore, causing discontentment among the Indian troops. Moreover, Japan did not positively respond to the Indian mission. The height of distrust was reached when N.S. Gill, an officer of the INA's espionage department, was arrested by the Japanese from the residence of Mohan Singh; at this, Mohan Singh ordered to disband the INA, resulting into his own arrest and exile to Pulau Ubin. Many of the Indian troops, who chose to revert to as POW, were sent to labour camps in New Guinea subsequently. Rash Behari Bose tried to patch up between the Indian Independence League and the Indian National Army, but to no avail.

The INA under Mohan Singh, also known as the First Indian National Army, was partly used in espionage missions in India and Burma with varying degree of success, especially in breeding discontentment among the Royal British Indian Army troops. Let us not forget that about this time, Gandhiji's call for 'Do or Die' had changed the political scenario in India. Its impact was seen on Britain when it imposed a ban on any news from reaching its troops from unauthorised sources. The anti-Japanese attitude on part of the Indian leadership was also evident during the Quit India Movement of 1942 when Gandhiji had warned Japan to keep off its hands. His words are historic when he said to the Japanese, "Make no mistake. You will be sadly disillusioned if you believe that you will receive a willing welcome from India."

This may also be noted in this connection that an army constituting ex-Royal British Indian Army personnel and Italians previously residing in India had been raised in Italy too. It was, however, chiefly propagandist by nature and did not find much acceptance among the Indian troops widely, so it did not last more than a few months in 1942.

* * * *

It was 10 August, 1942. Nambiar entered the cabin and wished Bose.

"Yes, Nambiar, what is going on?"

"I have some good news, Sir."

"What is that? These days, good news comes at a premium," Bose seemed to be a little disappointed. In fact, he had still been waiting to be transported to Japan despite the fact that his meeting with Hitler had taken place well over two months and a half back. Whenever he tried to contact the foreign office, he was not being given any concrete assurance. The situation was tricky to the extent that he had thought of slipping away from Germany stealthily as he had done it from his house arrest in Calcutta, but it could not have been so easy. Moreover, any such effort could have impeded Japanese sympathy too, as Germany and Japan were acting in collaboration during the Second World War.

Much water had flown in the Ganga ever since Bose had escaped from Calcutta in January 1941. The Indian National Congress gave tacit support to the British in its war 'against fascism', though it had a number of members who wanted to start a movement, because in September 1939, the resolution of Wardha meeting had expressed support to Britain for its war effort for grant of freedom in return; but it was rebuffed. Gandhiji did not want to seek to raise 'an independent India from the ashes of Britain'. As the British wanted to extract more of resources from India to contribute in its war, it imposed heartless taxes and other prohibitions to the extent of harassing people. This was leading to a situation where the people could rise in revolt. Moreover, Japan was threatening India's invasion. It was the fear of this revolt that the Cripps Mission was planned in March 1942. Headed by Stafford Cripps, the Leader of the House of Commons, this mission arrived in India to negotiate with the Congress to obtain total cooperation during the war, but in return, it did not offer any thing substantive which amounted to independence. The mission did not accept the key demand of a timetable of self-government, it only said that it could think of it only after cessation of hostilities. The two important proposals from it were the granting of dominion status to India and giving the princely states a choice whether to join the Indian Union or not. It also discreetly acceded to the demand for Pakistan. Obviously, this could not be acceptable to the Indian leadership. These proposals were termed as 'too little, too late'. Gandhiji said about its proposals, "It is a post-dated cheque on a crashing bank." Gandhiji also remarked in his article in the *Harijan* on 10 May, 1942: "The presence of the British in India is an invitation to Japan to invade India. Their withdrawal removes that bait." So, at the Bombay session of the All-India Congress Committee held on 8 August, 1942, Gandhiji gave the call for the Quit India Movement, demanding an end to the British rule in India. He gave a call for 'Do or Die'. People immediately erupted in protest. It spread like a wildfire. With this started the British suppression, beginning with the arrest of all Indian political leaders.

"Yes, Nambiar, give me the good news, hurry up," said Bose, a little impatiently.

"Here is the news," said Nambiar showing Bose an article in the newspaper. Bose's eyes shone on seeing the heading, 'Gandhi vows to throw the British out'. The news story was about the Quit India Movement in which Gandhiji had given a call for 'Do or Die'.

Bose hurriedly read through the news, nodded his head as if talking to himself, and then said, "Had I been in India at this hour!"

Nambiar knew Bose to be quite opposed to Gandhiji, so he was amazed at this reaction. He said, "You still have sympathy for Gandhiji, do you?"

"Yes, why not? He remains greatest of our leaders. Gandhiji should have started this movement at the time when this Second World War had erupted. Better late than never."

"But Gandhiji would never like what we are doing here," said Nambiar.

"That's right, but by giving the call for 'Do or Die', he has come quite close to our way of working," said Bose.

"What do you propose to do now?"

"I wish I could be with him at this juncture, but that's not possible. Still he needs my support," said Bose. "Do one thing, ask the technicians to come and record my speech over the radio."

"Yes, Sir," said Nambiar, before walking out.

Bose sat down to write the important points of his speech.

* * * *

Time was ticking by, and now it was the month of December. Bose was in constant touch with Japan. He was enthusiastic about the formation of the Indian Independence

League and the Indian National Army. His joy knew no bounds when he received an invitation from Rash Behari Bose for heading the INA.

"How do you view this invitation?" asked Nambiar.

"I don't think our plans can be realised in Germany," said Bose, thoughtfully. "It should be Asia where I should be."

"But do you think the Germans will allow you to slip away?" Nambiar sounded sceptical.

"Hitler promised to me that he would help me, but I doubt if people in the Gestapo are sincere," said Bose.

"They have kept an eye over every movement of ours, but now they seem to have intensified their watch."

"We have to take risks."

"What do you propose to do then?"

"Let me see, just send for Abid, I think the Japanese should help us out of this ordeal, we can't stay here like sitting ducks anymore," said Bose.

Nambiar went out and returned with Abid a few minutes later. He was in his Indian Legion uniform. "Good morning, Sir," said Abid in a loud voice saluting him.

"I suppose you have good clothes other than this uniform too," said Bose with a thin smile on his lips.

"Not very good, but I can do with them," said Abid in his characteristic smile. He was quite frank with Bose.

"You may have to move out of Germany at a short notice," said Bose. "You should be ready even at a minute's notice."

"Yes, Sir," said Abid. "Where do you plan to send me? For a pilgrimage?"

"There can be no greater pilgrimage than the mission I have planned to send you," said Bose. "You can go now."

Abid saluted and exited. Nambiar kept waiting for any instructions, and when Bose did not speak for a while, Nambiar said, "You seem to have finalised some plan."

"A plan is certainly there, but we have to see how it can be executed. I have to be in the theatre of war sooner than later," said Bose in a firm voice.

"What happens to your family in your absence?" said Nambiar.

"The risk is massive, but I am sure I would return with flying colours," said Bose. "You may leave now."

Nambiar went out and Bose sank in his chair thinking about Emilie, his wife and Anita, his daughter. Bose's passion for national movement for freedom had left him with little time to think about his family life. He got this opportunity in 1930s. He was now reflecting over the situation by which he happened to come into contact with Emilie.

* * * *

The political atmosphere in India was completely charged up with the 1929 declaration of complete Swaraj as the goal. Gandhiji had put 11 demands before the government and warned that the Civil Disobedience Movement would be started if these demands were not met. Two important demands included to release all political prisoners and abolition of the CID (Criminal Investigation Department), which had been a tool of harassing Indian politicians. As was expected, the British government paid no heed to these demands.

The Congress authorised Gandhiji to start the Movement. On 12 March, 1930, Gandhiji set out on the historic Dandi March from the Sabarmati Ashram in Ahmedabad with 78 followers for Dandi, a small village on the west coast, to break the Salt Law. Initially, the government looked at this march indignantly, but when the followers swelled to thousands, getting reception en route and spreading the message of fraternity, unity and khadi, the government was alarmed. Covering a distance of approximately 310 km over 25 days, Gandhiji arrived at Dandi. He picked up a handful of salt from the evaporated seawater and thus defied the Salt Law. It had massive repercussions across the country. People defied the law at various places, made salt, boycotted foreign goods and attempted the closure of wine shops. The government came down heavy on the protesters, who continued to protest peacefully despite raining batons, and courted arrest willingly. The movement spread from the north to the south to the northwest. The government responded with imprisonments. All important Congress and other leaders were arrested, but the Civil Disobedience Movement continued unabated.

When the Indian people were not satisfied with the Government of India Act, 1919, the British government constituted the Simon Commission, under the chairmanship of Sir John Simon, to report on the working of the reforms under the act. As all seven members of the commission were British, the Congress boycotted it when it arrived in 1928. It was during one such protest against the commission that Lala Lajpat Rai was caned, leading to his death, finally leading to the hanging of Bhagat Singh, Rajguru and Sukhdev in 1931.

The report of the Simon Commission was published in May 1930. It recommended a complete responsible government and making ministers responsible to the legislatures, but the Indian leaders and people remained firm on their demands. The British government held the First Round Table Conference in November 1930–January 1931, but the Congress decided to boycott it demanding the release of all political prisoners and amendment to the Salt Law. The government heeded, so the Congress decided to attend the Second Round Table Conference in September–December 1931. Gandhiji attended it as the sole representative of the Congress, but he returned disappointed. Just a couple of weeks earlier, the Labour Party had lost power to the Democrat Party in England, resulting into Lord Willingdon becoming the Viceroy of India in place of Lord Irwin. On the very first day of the conference, Gandhiji was told by the Secretary of State for India, Sir Samuel Hoare that India could not be given freedom, nor colonial self-rule. He even refused to accept Gandhiji as the representative of India. The

Third Round Table Conference, held towards the closing months of 1932, was boycotted by the Congress in view of the negative attitude of the British government.

When Gandhiji returned with empty hands, the entire country was shocked, but Bose was one of those who felt that this was bound to occur. He felt that Gandhiji could not face the pressure as the sole representative, he should have been accompanied by more nationalists. Issuing a press statement, Bose pointed out that Gandhiji's saintliness, humility and excessive respect shown for the opponents brought down his effectiveness. He concluded that had Gandhiji talked in hard terms like Hitler, Mussolini or Stalin, Britain would have realised his importance and knelt down.

On return from England, Gandhiji gave a call for restarting the Civil Disobedience Movement, which started from 1 January, 1931. The government was, however, ready to meet any such eventuality. It ordered to arrest all 'troublemakers'. The name of Bose led the rest. He was arrested the following day. In two months, thousands of people were arrested. Cane-charges were the order of the day. The Congress was declared an unlawful organisation and all types of processions, protests and assemblies had been prohibited. However, the Indian people came to the fore in larger numbers; they engaged themselves in burning bonfires of foreign clothes and goods, picketing of shops selling British goods and taking out processions and holding meetings of different sizes. The entire atmosphere was quite inflammatory. As all important leaders were put behind bars, the Movement gradually waned.

The British were not content with all these brutalities. They wanted to take a step that would prevent the Indians from raising their head any time in the future; it was to follow their effective policy of 'divide and rule'; earlier, they had sowed seeds of animosity between Hindus and Muslims, and now they decided to fragment the Hindu community. Under the plan, Prime Minister MacDonald announced a controversial policy, better known as 'communal award'. Under it, the untouchables were regarded as a distinct community and were to be given separate representation in the legislatures; they could vote only for the untouchable candidates, and had no right to vote to candidates of any other castes. This step was sure to fragment the society into several small segments, each nursing selfish intents.

Seeing the negative intentions woven into this step, Gandhiji protested and went on a fast unto death. Incarcerated in jail, Bose came to know from the messages he received about this. He praised Gandhiji and said that his fast had acquainted the world with the administrative calamity that had befallen the country. Praising the courage shown by Gandhiji, Bose said that this internal conflict was given importance to the extent of staking his life to peril.

The prolonged fast deteriorated Gandhiji's health, so a pact was reached between high-caste and low-caste Hindus. It was agreed that the common electorates would be retained but 1148 seats would be reserved for the depressed classes in the provincial legislative councils as well as 18 percent of the seats in the Central Legislative Council. The

British government accepted this agreement and withdrew the communal award. Gandhiji gave up his fast, but later observed another 21-day-long fast to purify his soul.

Bose, on the other hand, was suffering from ill-health in the jail. He had been lodged in a small, dusty, damp cell, with little provisions for safety against heat, cold or rain. His illness started to grow serious; the symptoms of tuberculosis could be seen in him. The government was not in favour of releasing him as it was aware of the powerful impact he had on the masses; so, it shifted him to Jabalpur Central Jail for medical treatment. The doctors examined him there and recommended to shift him to some warm place for treatment. The situation in North India was quite volatile in view of the Civil Disobedience Movement in 1932; and the government feared that revolutionaries could break the jail to secure his release as he was also associated with the Naujawan Bharat Sabha, a revolutionary organisation. So, Bose was shifted to Madras, but it served no purpose, so he was sent to Bhowali Sanatorium in United Provinces, and then to Lucknow.

All these transfers from one jail to another did not serve much purpose, as Bose's condition continued to grow from bad to worse, to the extent that the jail doctors feared loss of his life. The medical officer wrote to the jail superintendent that the chief cause of his illness was lack of necessary facilities and hygiene, and his life could be saved by change of environment and better medical treatment. He also warned that the authorities would have to embrace themselves for any calamity in case due attention was not paid to him.

The British government knew that it could not play with the life of Bose, as he was endeared to the people on par with Gandhiji, still it was not ready to release him as it feared that Bose would not care for his life and would join the national movement which was in a critical state then. It was taking precaution of censoring any information regarding his health, but still some news filtered out leading to wild conjectures. The Indian people were not unaware of the atrocities that were being meted out to Bose in the jail, and when they came to know that Bose's condition had deteriorated greatly to the extent that he could die, anguish spread; they could not allow their courageous and brave leader to die the death of a jackal. The demand for his release was raised in the form of protests and processions; public meetings were held to censure the government; and strikes were observed. When the government found that it could not withstand the mounting pressure, it gave in, but with a clause to play it safe. It said, "If Bose agreed to go abroad on his own expense, he could be released from jail."

At first, Bose did not want to leave his country when she needed him the most, but going abroad was better than dying in a dark, dingy cell. It could have other benefits too. He could spread the awareness how the British were unleashing atrocities on the Indian people, seeking assistance from the Indians settled abroad. He consented to his going abroad after he had made up his mind what he was to do there.

The way Bose was made to board a steamer to Europe without allowing him to meet any one here showed that the government was scared of his grand personality more than any one else's. He was ill and weak, yet he seemed to have massive influence in the country.

Bose first landed in Italy and then made for Vienna in Austria. He regained his health at Dr. Ferth's Sanatorium. He wanted to return to India, but the situation was not suitable. He could not have taken the pressure of joining the national movement as yet, but he decided to do his bit while being out of the country. In the same sanatorium, Bose came across Vithalbhai Patel, brother of Sardar Vallabhbhai Patel. He too was connected with the national movement and had taken part in protests against the British government; he was more inclined to revolutionary activism rather than Gandhi's way of protests hinging on Satyagraha and fasts. He openly said that the British should be replied in their own language which they understood well. The two shared common sentiments so far as the freedom of the country was concerned; they often discussed the prevailing political circumstances in the country and what the European circumstances had in store for the world.

When Gandhiji suspended the Civil Disobedience Movement and undertook the fast for self-purification, Bose was not comfortable with this idea. He issued a joint statement with Vithalbhai Patel. It said that latest suspension of the Civil Disobedience Movement was heading to a failure. It said that Gandhiji had failed as a political leader, and now was the right time when the Congress organisation was reformed according to the new methods and new principles.

As Gandhiji was not able to formulate effective long-term plan, it would be injustice to him to expect of him to make new plans. It would be better for the Congress to undertake this complete change itself, else a new party would have to be formed out of the Congress which would constitute the reformative elements.

Bose knew that his criticism of Gandhiji could not be taken kindly, still he was of the view that the statement was against the passive resistance of Gandhiji as, in his view, India had reached a level where active policies were the need of the hour. He opined that the failure of the Round Table Conferences had proved that dialogue never changed the history; its only alternative is armed rebellion. The sons of India were now ready to shed blood, whether their own or that of the enemy. His opinion was going to set a stage for India's freedom movement.

Vithalbhai Patel was so impressed by Bose's personality and ideals that he named him the successor to his moveable and immoveable property. Before his death in October 1933; Patel wrote in his will: "I have seen that patriot, he is infused with unshakable faith and is bent upon struggling for India's freedom without any compromise. All my property should be given to him; he is free to utilise this money for the progress of India in any way he deems fit."

However, Sardar Vallabhbhai Patel challenged the will in the court. The case ran for six years after which Bose's claim to his property was struck down. Later, Vallabhbhai assigned this property to Gandhiji for social work.

In December 1933, the Congress of Oriental Studies was set up in Italy. Several thinkers were invited to deliver lectures in its inaugural programme; Bose was one of the invitees, especially in view of his support to socialism. Mussolini, the then Prime Minister of Italy who had set up a totalitarian state, was also present. He was fascinated by Bose's powerful speech. He saw a powerful leader in Bose, a leader who could defeat Britain to clinch power.

At the end of the meeting, Mussolini talked to him and posed a direct question, "Are you fully confident that India would be free soon?"

Nodding in the affirmative, Bose replied in a firm voice, "Yes, it would occur sooner than later."

"What do you favour: reform or revolution?"

"In my view, revolution is inevitable to get the country free, without it, a dream of freedom is like begging. The concept of reform can be bloomed in a free country, else it is meaningless in slavery."

Mussolini was greatly impressed by this reply. He tapped his shoulder and said, "If India's leadership lies in powerful hands like yours, there are strong chances of it getting freedom quite soon."

This meeting had opened avenues for thinking that assistance of European countries could be got if planned properly. During his return journey to Vienna, Bose was thinking on a new line of approach to the problem.

* * * *

Bose didn't have much to do during his sojourn in Austria. Earlier in the company of Chittranjan Das, he had emerged as a writer and editor for a daily named *Banglar Katha.* It was way back in 1920s. Now when he had time at his disposal, he decided to put it to good use, and this was how he started writing. Now, pen was his companion. He chose the Indian freedom movement as the topic of his writing. He continued to write and in some time, a large pile of papers was ready with him. He decided to shape it into a book, but for this, he needed the services of a secretary who possessed a working knowledge of English and could typewrite and put the book into order. He sent out the word that he was looking for one. It was how he was introduced to Emilie Schenkl through a mutual friend. She too was looking for a job as, due to the Great Depression, Europe was reeling under economic pressure. Bose found Emilie a very intelligent, hardworking, kind, tolerant and emotional person. These days, Bose was not keeping well physically, and she came forward to look after his health too. Her support had positive effect on Bose, both as writer and as person. He overcame his illness. Due to this profound service, Bose wrote that he had no hesitation in admitting that it would have been a hard nut to crack to complete the book without active cooperation of Emilie; he described her contribution as commendable.

By this time, Bose had never spared a thought to his love life, but when he came across Emilie, he was attracted to her. On the other hand, she too was fascinated by his grand views and personality. They fell in love, but Bose never forgot his original objective for which he had hired *Emilie*. He completed his book, titled The *Indian Struggle*. It was published in November 1934. This book dealt with political circumstances prevailing in India; it also reviewed almost all popular leaders of the time. He had taken an objective style of writing, tending to note down the facts and expressed few views in it.

This book brought about an upheaval in Europe. Until now, people outside India little knew about the actual conditions prevailing in India. What they knew about India was through the writings of the British or European writers who hid more than they revealed; they talked more of the Maharajas and snakes and elephants rather than the social and political life of people. This book sought to bring reality to light. In this book, Bose noted that the struggle started by the Indians is not the one in which only a few castes, communities or people are involved to realise their selfish ends; rather it is the struggle for national pride, self-respect, self-dependence and freedom; it was a struggle against colonialism and imperialism. India was struggling to achieve freedom, and this struggle is being contributed to by every citizen. It is the collective struggle of the nation, in which different communities and castes have come together. He noticed that the Indians were little bothered about what the world thought about them; they had set before them a goal and were now ready to sacrifice anything they possessed. He concluded in his book that the British atrocities in India were to last only a few days more, the time was not far when the forehead of India would be daubed with victory and when it would be identified in the world with respect and dignity.

Bose presented the Indian point of view very firmly, acquainting the western countries how cruelly the British were dealing with them. As expected, the book sold like hot cakes in Europe. *The Manchester Guardian*, a prominent English paper, noted that it was the most interesting and impressive book ever written by an Indian politician on Indian politics. If it is compared with the books written by the generation of writers like Lala Lajpat Rai, it would be explicit that Indian political thought is on the path of maturity. The newspaper further wrote that the book has been written by the youngest of the three most popular leaders of India. It has dealt with Gandhi a bit harshly, but it is clear from the context that it is not born out of animosity towards him. Bose has also included other aspects of India including evolution of socialism, labour movement and trade union movement; his profound interest in them have made the book interesting and worth reading. Such reviews were carried in almost all newspapers and magazines.

The book now encouraged people to look at Bose and other political leaders in India with curiosity. The book had found recognition as a high quality book on politics. Even the readers in England were not untouched. A record sale was recorded there.

The British government had seen how the book had evinced interest among the people in Europe, and it was making inroads in India, despite the fact that it was not yet launched there. As expected, the British government banned the book in India; however, it could not prevent its entry in India. The ban only evoked more curiosity among the people.

* * * *

Love is a delicate experience, a feeling so profound, an emotion beyond description, a sentiment directly linked with the heart; this can be felt by a person who attaches importance to the mind as well as the heart. It is a term which is simple to feel, pure to think and complicated to explain. It is the bliss that jingles all the strings of the mind, heart and body; in its subtle form, nothing is greater than this. Love is devoid of all selfish interests, it is woven by noble qualities of the head and the heart; it is the invisible bond that unites people; man without it is nothing more than a beast.

Close association with Emilie awakened Bose to the sublime feelings of love. She entered his life as a proficient secretary with a good command over English, but her other qualities came to be revealed during this course. The two came to like each other, and then fell in love. This came through mutual understanding; they respected each other's sentiments as well as views; they possessed similar philosophical views; despite their difference in races, countries and colours of skin. They felt intensely for each other.

* * * *

During his sojourn in Europe, after he recovered from his illness, he sought to visit different countries in order to study their different organisations, and meet important philosophers, thinkers and politicians; he wanted to learn from them how he could make the Indian freedom movement more effective. This touring gave him an opportunity to set right the rumours that the British had spread about India and the circumstances prevailing there. He also studied the constitutions in different countries. The two things he was most impressed by were the political system in Italy and the Irish underground movement. He was also impressed by the policy of neutrality as followed by Turkey which was now attempting to revamp the existing system into a modern structure such that other countries would not interfere in its internal affairs. He learnt from Italy that India needed a political party which can not only endeavour for India's freedom, but also construct the National Constitution and implement the scheme for national reconstruction. He advocated two responsibilities of the political party: to establish a military organisation and reconstruction of the nation after freedom.

All these interactions helped Bose to shape his ideas; he was gradually becoming more mature with time. On the occasion of the Congress's golden jubilee in 1935, Bose wrote that there was little hope left in the nonviolent movement as it had failed to evoke the British conscience, all such hopes have been belied. He noted that the Satyagraha had failed to realise its goal, and now was the time when the Congress should introspect honestly. He advised the Congress to establish a foreign wing that should get in touch with other countries and also inform the international community about India on different international fora.

* * * *

The year was 1936. Bose had recovered from his illness to a great extent, though he was not yet fully fit. He was growing restless to return to India to take active part in the national movement. He had done all that he could do in Europe and he felt that it was the right time to return to India.

Bose was sitting on the floor with crossed legs. He often assumed this posture whenever he was in deep thought.

"What are you doing?" said Emilie entering the room and putting on the light. "Meditating?"

"No, not meditating," said Bose looking into the vacuum. "It is high time I should be in India."

"You are not yet physically fit, are you?"

"Of course, but I can't keep sitting like a duck. The time is ticking by, I have to take action, I have to free my people from the foreign yoke," said Bose in an emotional tone.

"I respect your sentiments, but I fear you would be imprisoned as soon as you climb down the ship in India," Emilie was concerned.

"I can't say, but there are strong possibilities of it," said Bose firmly, "still I want to be among my people. My motherland is calling me. I have to repay her debt."

Emilie sat down beside him. After a pause, she handed him a letter. "Here is a letter from India," she said.

Bose tore open the letter. It was from the Indian National Congress, written by Jawaharlal Nehru. He read it hurriedly.

"Look, Emilie, my love for my people is not one-sided, my people also want me there," said Bose showing the letter.

"What does it say?"

"I have been invited to attend the Congress session at Lucknow," said Bose.

"I don't find this much encouraging," Emilie argued. In fact, she was afraid that Bose might leave forever, she wanted to be in his company though the two had not yet married. She looked into Bose's eyes and said, "Don't you agree that the Congress is inactive at this time; it has given up its resistance against the government ordinances. And to top it all, the government would put you in jail straightway; your very going there would become meaningless."

"Still, I think I must go," said Bose.

"I think otherwise. I think you should stay here and work for your goal from here. People are already giving a sympathetic hearing to your cause. You are not keeping well," said Emilie. Bose could see her eyes becoming moist.

"I respect your sentiments," said Bose holding her hand affectionately. "I can't stay back any more. I must go."

In March 1936, Bose took Emilie's leave for Bombay.

"Will we meet again?" asked Emilie.

"I don't know yet, but you will ever reside in my mind and soul," said Bose in an emotional tone.

Bose departed, but he was destined to meet Emilie not very long after.

* * * *

Bose arrived in Bombay the following month, and as it was rightly feared by Emilie, he was taken into custody and lodged in the Yerawada Jail. He had returned to India to attend the Congress session at Lucknow, but he could not. He of course sent a message to Nehru, "Keep the flag of freedom flying high."

Despite Bose being imprisoned, he was made a member of the Congress Working Committee in absentia. The Congress also tried for his release, but without any perceptible result. When all efforts to get him released failed, Nehru started a movement from 10 May, 1936, declaring this day as Subhas Day. He gave a call for a general strike, leading to cessation of work in shops, factories and elsewhere. People took to streets, and people's anguish burst out in the form of terrible flames at some places. Within ten days, the movement became fierce. The government was hard pressed; seeing no option before it, it released Bose from jail but put him under house arrest. But the people wanted him completely free; in addition, his old illness had resurfaced. Helpless, the government ordered his release on 17 March, 1937, unconditionally. The news found prominent place in the newspapers across the country, sending a wave of happiness everywhere. He was given a public reception on 6 April, 1937, in which a large number of organisations honoured him.

The doctors advised Bose to head to hills for recovery, so he first went to Dalhousie, but finding no respite from disease, he once again left for Vienna, arriving there on 18 November, 1937. He was sure that the company of Emilie would heal his illness.

"I am back, Emilie," Bose surprised Emilie.

"I knew you would come for sure," said Emilie. "You're sick again."

"Yes, but I'm feeling better in your company."

"Didn't I tell you that you would be imprisoned the moment you land in Bombay?"

"You did, but my motherland needs me."

"Now I won't allow you to go any more."

"I may be ill, but I am not out. My first love is for my country. How can I live here peacefully when my people are suffering?"

"I want you to bind me in your love," said Emilie.

"You reside in my heart."

"Shall we marry?"

"Yes, we can marry, but promise you won't be an obstacle in my path."

"Any wife would want her husband to be with her at all times, but I wouldn't stop you from serving your first love."

"You have won my heart, you have won me."

"Let's then go forward with our marriage. I want it to be held as per the Hindu rites."

The marriage ceremony was hurriedly arranged. An indologist performed the rituals. Emilie is said to have objected to the absence of a Hindu Brahmin, but Bose convinced her that the term 'Brahmin' means a scholar, and the indologist present there was one.

The marriage remained a secret, as it was not registered, nor were any people present there. There were no witnesses to the marriage, nor any evidence. The marriage took place for sure, but it remained a matter of conjecture for people.

This time Bose did not stay in Vienna for long. He did not pass this time lying on the bed; he took Emilie's help to write his second book: *An Indian Pilgrim*. He recovered soon, so he first went to England to meet politicians, philosophers and thinkers in order to convince them about the actual state of affairs in India. He got information that he had been nominated as President of the Indian National Congress. He grew emotional and restless; he wanted to be in India as soon as possible. The time for session was round the corner, so he left Britain and arrived in India on 24 January, 1938. He was elected its President in 1938, but soon he came in conflict with Gandhiji. It resulted in his abdicating the high post the next year despite his being elected again.

* * * *

February 1943. Bose was at his desk writing something when Emilie entered. She was a little agitated. Bose asked, "What's the matter, Emilie?"

"I've heard that your plan for departure is final."

"Yes, you're right. I've recorded my speeches for broadcast on radio during my absence, so no one would know about my travelling."

"How are you going?"

"Under the sea, by U-boat."

"What, by U-boat, you mean submarine? Are you mad? Who has ever heard of such a long journey under the sea? I can't allow you to take this journey."

"Don't worry, Emilie, nothing would happen to me. No harm would come to me until my India is under the foreign yoke."

"I am not sure. I can't allow you to go like this. Why don't you ask them for an aeroplane or ship?"

"That is not at all safe," said Bose trying to convince his wife. "I can travel under the sea without being noticed by the enemy. If I travel by air or by ship, I'm sure to come under an Allied attack."

"Oh!" Emilie stood rooted to her ground for a while. She walked out and soon returned with their daughter, Anita in her arms. Bose took the baby in his hands and pressed her to his chest in fatherly affection.

"How pretty you look playing with her!" said Emilie. Her emotions clearly expressed that she was not comfortable with his going away.

"I love you, my darling Anita," said Bose kissing her rosy cheek. "Who is the man in the world who would not want to be in the company of his little daughter? But I bear a greater responsibility on my shoulders."

"You are going on a risky mission."

"Yes, risky of course, but I'm sure to return. When I return next time, I would live with you forever, because I would have accomplished my mission by that time."

"When will you reach Asia?"

"If all goes well, within three weeks."

"What happens of us?"

Bose found it hard to convince Emilie. He tapped on her shoulder and pointing to the letter on the table, he said, "I've written this letter to my family in Calcutta. This will tell them that you are my wife and that I have a lovely daughter."

Emilie kept standing blankly for some time before saying, "Is it not possible for you to register our marriage?"

"Here, in Germany?"

"Yes, why not? At least, we'll have a record of sort," said Emilie.

"I've written this letter, you'll be accepted in my family," said Bose looking into her eyes.

"I'm not much worried about your family. The foreign office people here think that we're not married and I stick to you to get all these facilities. They think that I am using my liaison with you to live an especially comfortable life in these hard times of war." This long dialogue seemed to have tired her.

"Don't be agitated," Bose tried to assuage her feelings. "I'll do my best."

Bose did try to get the marriage registered, but without success. In fact, it was owing to Hitler's thinking that the Europeans were racially superior, and his policy that if a German married a non-European, his or her citizenship would be forfeited.

Bose bid adieu to Emilie and his little daughter on 8 February, 1943. At this time he said, "I'm sure to come back soon. Wait wouldn't be long, be assured." But will he really return?

As it turned out, Bose never returned. The couple had stayed together for less than three years. Emilie worked to bring up her daughter. Bose's brother, Sarat Chandra met her in Austria later, but she never visited India. She died in 1996. She never talked of her relationship with Bose. Their relationship remained a mysterious one, and their marriage has been contested often.

* * * *

The War

Bose wanted to travel with his bunch of trusted officers with other arrangements to transfer his troops of the Indian Legion later, but Germany allowed only one person to accompany him. Bose chose Abid Hasan, who was serving as his private secretary in the Indian Legion. They first travelled to Kiel by train and then boarded a German submarine U-180. The information about his departure was kept completely confidential. The submarine sailed along Africa around the Cape of Good Hope to the southeast of Madagascar, where he was transferred to the Japanese submarine I-29, with the help of a rubber boat, for the remaining journey to imperial Japan. His journey remained uneventful despite the long time it took; of course, they came under bombing on one occasion, but slipped past safely. As the records go, this was the only civilian transfer between two submarines of two different nations during the Second World War.

Bose got off the submarine at Sabang, Indonesia, on 6 May, 1943. At the harbour, he was welcomed by the Japanese officials. From there he flew to Tokyo, stopping en route, and finally reached Tokyo on 16 May. The long voyage and journey was extremely risky, especially during those belligerent times, but Bose was ready to risk his life for the sake of his mission.

Bose studied the circumstances there and how far the imperialist Japan could help him realise his goal of India's freedom. He also met, on 10 June, 1943, General Hideki Tojo, the Prime Minister of Japan. The meeting was scheduled only for twenty minutes, but General Tojo was so impressed by Bose's personality that the meeting lasted well beyond the scheduled time. He discussed with him several issues in order to know more of him. Tojo is reported to have said to his advisor about Bose: "This Indian is undoubtedly great; there can be none more capable than him who can lead the Indian National Army."

Bose also attended the Japanese legislature, the National Diet, which expressed support to Bose and his cause and criticised Britain's atrocities and brutal suppression.

Now, Bose had obtained Japan's support, and did no more need to remain in hiding. He called a press conference on 19 June, 1943, and issued a statement. In it he said how the British had not kept their word after the First World War, and now they could not be trusted. The Indians had been waiting for an opportunity like this which the Second World War had presented, so they were embracing themselves for liberating themselves from the British shackles. He said that the Indians were ready to shed blood and were ready to make any sacrifices that might be needed to preserve freedom. Sword must face the sword.

This statement took the world by storm. His location was known to the world now, while the Indians cheered that their saviour was making all-out efforts for their liberation.

* * * *

Bose arrived in Singapore, in July 1943.

On 4 July, the atmosphere in the Cathay Cinema Hall, Singapore, was jubilant and optimistic. It was going to witness a historic moment, it was ready to leave the marks of history on the sands of time. The troops of the Indian National Army stood erect waiting for Bose to arrive and assume the command. Until now, most of the troops consisted of the prisoners of war, but they did not make a sizeable army, as they were only about 8,000 of them. Efforts needed to be made in order to increase the size of the INA so that the Japanese as well as the British would take this force somewhat seriously. For its supplies and equipment, the INA had to be fully dependent on the Japanese authorities.

Bose had arrived here on the invitation of the Japanese and Rash Behari Bose to revive the dormant INA. In the hall were present Rash Behari Bose, the chief of the Indian Independence League; representatives of the Japanese army command led by Hideki Tojo; immigrant Indian nationalists and officials of the INA.

As soon as Bose appeared on the stage with Hideki Tojo, the entire place reverberated with the slogans of 'Bharat Mata Ki Jai'. The nationalists seemed to be very enthusiastic. When the slogans pacified, Rash Behari Bose took to the mike. Welcoming the guests on the stage, he addressed the gathering: "Today before you is present Subhas Chandra Bose who needs no introduction, you know him well enough. He is the true son of the motherland and is a brave warrior. Today, in your presence, I relieve myself of my post and propose to appoint him as the chairman of the Indian Independence League of East Asia. Until now I had kept the sacred flame of freedom struggle in my hands. Besides, I also declare him to be the Commander-in-Chief of the INA. I wish him all success."

With these words, Bose took to the mike among the sky-rending roar of the slogans. He addressed: "The time has come when you need to come forward for independence of the country. This effort would need discipline, unity and sacrifice."

Concluding his speech, Bose gave a call for now famously known as 'Chalo Dilli' (On to Delhi).

* * * *

The handing-taking over ceremony being over, Bose was now in his new avatar. He was in the new uniform, though he did not take any rank. As he walked out surrounded by his officers and volunteers, he was saluted. Bose raised his right hand to his forehead and looked to the man who had saluted him. "You!" he could not suppress his amazement at seeing the face. "You, here!" exclaimed Bose.

It was Subhas who had met him first in Peshawar and then in Afghanistan.

"I think you now need me," said Subhas with a twinkle in his face.

"Yes, I need you and thousands of others who will help realise freedom of the country," said Bose emphatically. "Follow me."

"Neta Saheb," said Subhas, "I would like to tell you one thing."

Abid Hasan was walking next to them. He interrupted, "This address is fine, shall I amend it a little?"

"Which term are you talking about?" asked Bose.

"Neta Saheb, I think we should make it Netaji," said Abid.

"I suppose that is the fittest appellation for him, Netaji Ki Jai," Subhas said loudly attracting everybody's attention.

* * * *

The following day, at the army headquarter in Singapore, Bose announced the establishment of the Indian National

Army in a ceremonial parade. He took the salute and addressed the parade and those present there. He expressed confidence that the fledgling army would be able to free India from the British yoke and would also construct future national consciousness of the free nation of India. He laid emphasis on Ittefaq or unity, Ittemad or self-belief and Qurbani or sacrifice. Without these, he said, freedom of the country could not be preserved to eternity. He exhorted them that under the prevailing situations, he could give nothing but hunger, thirst, poverty and death; but if he was cooperated with, he would lead them to victory and liberty. He concluded his speech with the contribution of women in the freedom struggle. He said that India had a tradition of women fighters ever since the ancient times. He sought their cooperation and said that they should march with men shoulder-to-shoulder. Without them, the Azad Hind Fauz would remain incomplete.

It was here that the Tricolour was first hoisted in this march past. It was much like the present Indian Tricolour, with the only change in the middle white stripe which had a Charkha or spinning wheel in place of the present-day Chakra or wheel.

This was how the Rani Jhansi Regiment was formed, led by Captain Lakshmi Swaminathan. The Japanese officers objected to the training of women saying that they had no tradition of women participating in the battle. Bose was clear what he wanted. He replied that the Rani Jhansi Regiment was not to become a showpiece, rather it would be sent to the battle front to take part in actual fighting. He also said that as the Commander-in-Chief of the INA, he had authority to set up organisations like that.

After announcement to the founding of the INA, Bose chaired the meeting of his officers. He was introduced to his officers by Lt. Col. Bhonsale. The important INA officers present there included Sehgal, Aziz Mohammad Khan, Chatterjee, Habib ur Rahman, Inayat Kiani, Shahnawaz Khan, in addition to Anand Sahay as representative of the IIL and S.A. Ayer as his secretary.

Bose took his seat round the table with his officials and passed initial instructions regarding administration, training, organisation and general policies. He also intimated the officers that he was in the process of declaring the setting up of the provisional government of free India. He also instructed them to embrace themselves for all aspects of civilian administration like currency, supplies, security, court, civil code, postage stamps and foreign relations. He said that a number of governments were ready to recognise his government.

* * * *

As Bose stepped out of the chamber, he found Subhas who promptly saluted.

"I thought you would attend the meeting," said Bose.

"I hold no post as of now," said Subhas.

"I'll solve that now. Now, you will be my secretary on par with Abid Hasan. And as he is a trained officer and is likely to leave to the front, you will take over the charge," said Bose.

"Thank you, Netaji."

The two started to walk. "Until then you have to do an important job."

"We are a small force as of now," said Subhas. "Nobody will take us seriously, nor can we do anything worthwhile in the war."

"You're right, we've got to expand our strength."

"Wherefrom will people come to join us?"

"This is the job I want to assign to you. There is about 30 lakh-strong Indian community in Malaya, Singapore and Burma. It is your job is to contact them and ask them to cooperate with men and money," said Bose. "We need both."

"Thank you for showing this trust," said Subhas. "It would be better if you inaugurate this campaign yourself and then I'll take over. But I have a doubt because most of these people are either plantation workers or shopkeepers. Will they ever make good soldiers?"

"Have no doubt about their potential; training will certainly make them good soldiers. They will not be ordinary soldiers who fight for their salary; they will be fighting for freedom. Okay for now, move to Burma and gather people for this purpose. I'll be there soon."

"Yes, Netaji," said Subhas before bowing out.

* * * *

Burma was liberated by Japan on 1 August, 1943. Japan immediately announced it a free state. Bose was invited to join the celebration. Addressing a conference in Rangoon, Bose said, “During its rule in India, the British government made a number of promises to Indians, which have remained only on paper. On the contrary, Prime Minister General Tojo has kept his word fully. However, I am sure that without India’s freedom, the Asian countries cannot be fully liberated.”

Burma borders India, so Bose was interested in locating the headquarters of his provisional government here. At first, the Burmese government was apprehensive, but later agreed to it with the condition that Bose would not interfere in its internal matters.

* * * *

Subhas entered the chamber and saluted, “Jai Hind, Netaji.”

“Jai Hind,” said Bose.

“Here is a letter for you. It seems to be a private one.”

Bose tore open the letter and read. It informed him of his mother’s death. He grew sad. Fighting for the motherland, he had forgotten the mother who had given him birth. His eyes grew moist. “O Mother,” murmured he, “I’m sure you would pardon this son; he is busy looking after the other mother.”

Subhas stood gazing at the changing demeanour of Bose. He asked, “There seems to be some news.”

"Yes, my mother..." Bose could not complete his statement. He seemed to have lost his firmness for which he was known. "Subhas, now time has come when we should march to India. Our motherland calls us. We are already late."

* * * *

21 October, 1943. A large assembly gathered, attended by about one thousand Indian representatives from East Asian countries. The resolution for setting up a provisional government, Azad Hind Government or Arzi Hukumat-e-Azad Hind was passed. Bose was nominated as its head. Taking an oath to the office, he proclaimed: "I, Subhas Chandra Bose, swear in the name of God that I would liberate 38 crore Indians and will fight this struggle until the last breath of my life. I shall ever remain a servant to India and will protect the welfare of my countrymen. It would be my supreme duty. I would be ever present to preserve the freedom of my country to the last drop of blood in my body."

The Provisional Government of Free India was instantly recognised by nine Axis states which included Germany, Japan, Italy, the Independent State of Croatia, Wang Jingwei regime in Nanjing, China, a provisional government of Burma, Manchukuo and Japanese-controlled Philippines. The Soviet Russia did not recognise it directly, but agreed to keep diplomatic contacts.

The setting up of the provisional government was like a ray of hope for millions of Indians back home. Though the Congress looked at this development with consternation, people were jubilant and hoped that their freedom was not far off.

Forming a government is a complex process. Bose immediately convened a council of his officers. He explained to them: "Keep in mind that ours is not a government of peaceful times. It is a committee overlooking struggles for freedom. The cabinet of the government will comprise of military officers and only a few civil officers. We are passing through the final stages of the war. Soon you will see the INA marching into India and then the struggle to take over Delhi will begin in right earnest. This movement will rest only after the British have been driven out of India and hoisting of the National Flag on the Viceroy's Building."

Bose also laid down broad objectives for which the cabinet and officers should work. He said that after the British were driven out, the confidence of the Indians would have to be won in order to set up a national government. He also instructed that they were moving towards providing all citizens of India religious freedom, equal rights and equal opportunities, and put India on the path to prosperity and progress.

Bose formed his 21-member cabinet comprising eight military officers from the INA, five civilian ministers, eight Indian representatives living in Southeast and East Asian countries. The important people to take charge included Captain Lakshmi Swaminathan as in-charge for the women organisation, S.A. Ayer as minister of the publication and propaganda department, Col. A.C. Chatterjee as finance minister and A.N. Sarkar as the legal advisor. Rash Behari Bose was the overall mentor and advisor.

* * * *

"What is your progress?" Bose asked Subhas.

"I have motivated people and many are ready to join us; Netaji, I think you need to address a rally after which they will all join us in large numbers," assured Subhas.

"Will they contribute with money too? We are in need of money, you know we cannot be fully dependent on the Japanese for many things," said Bose.

"Yes, Netaji, only you need to exhort people."

As if the people were waiting for Netaji's call, they competed with one another to contribute with young men to join the INA and with money and jewellery. Many of them sold their houses and other things to aid the noble cause. Bose and other officials received these contributions most thankfully, assuring them that this money would be put to the optimum use.

In a few days, a large number of people joined the INA. Its strength was now close to 45,000 men. Training was underway and the shortcomings in training and drill were overcome by the determination they displayed. They were all ready to sacrifice themselves. A training school for INA officers was set up under the command of Col Habib ur Rahman, and the Azad School was set up to impart short-term training to civilian recruits. Tokyo Boys, a team of

45 young Indians, chosen by Bose personally, was sent to Japan's Imperial Military Academy for training as fighter pilots.

The INA's first commitment was in the Japanese thrust towards Northeastern Indian frontiers along Manipur. The INA was divided into three main divisions: Gandhi Brigade or 2nd Guerilla Regiment, commanded by Col. Inayat Kiani; Azad Brigade or 3rd Guerilla Regiment, commanded by Col. Gulzara Singh; and Nehru Brigade or 4th Guerilla Regiment, commanded by Lt. Col. Gurbaksh Singh Dhillon. A fourth regiment, called Subhas Brigade, commanded by Col. Shahnawaz Khan, was created from the veterans of the other three brigades whose chief purpose was to undertake special operations, like laying ambushes and striking the core of the enemy. There was, in addition, a special operations group, called Bahadur, which was trained to operate behind enemy lines to give a 'shock treatment'. Thus, we can see that the provisional government had teeth to bite too, it was not a mere showpiece. The INA was declared to be the army of Azad Hind or Free India.

The equipment and resources with the INA were not sufficient, they were chiefly issued with arms and ammunition that the Japanese had captured from the British army. They did not have proper clothing and boots, and rations were very short-supplied. But the INA troops were motivated and determined; they were never scared of such constraints; before them lay the noblest of goals: liberty of their motherland.

* * * *

The INA, under the overall command of Netaji Bose, had to prove its worth as well as effectiveness. The advanced army headquarters were moved to Rangoon to effectively liaise with the forces.

On 23 October, 1943, Bose declared a war against Britain and the United States. On 24 October, he went on air declaring the war. He addressed the countrymen saying that the time had come when they must be united and take on the brutal British and vowed to fight with the British forces until the last drop in the body.

'Jai Hind' and 'Chalo Dilli' had become popular slogans in the INA as well as India. Indians were anxiously and eagerly waiting for the INA operations to begin.

"Is it the right time to start our operations, Netaji?" asked Subhas.

"Why, do you have a doubt?"

"Japan has started to face reverses in battles and Germany is also in a precarious position," said Subhas.

"That has certainly created difficulties for us. What do you suggest?"

"We should plan our operations such that we don't have to retreat despite the defeat of Japan or other Axis Powers," opined Subhas.

"Can that ever be possible?" wondered Bose.

"Instead of taking on the British army head on, we should rather concentrate on guerilla warfare. Secondly, we should encourage defections of Indian troops from the enemy," said Subhas.

"That's the idea, it will increase our strength, bring us required supplies and will also weaken the enemy," said Bose. His face was now shining with the possibility of a victory in the upcoming operations. He concluded, "And when our forces are in the Indian mainland, they will march towards the Gangetic plains, undertake guerilla operations living off the land and gain support from local population."

Subhas saluted and went out but returned a few minutes later.

"Netaji, Field Marshal Terauchi wants to see you," informed Subhas.

"Bring him in," said Bose.

The two shook hands and sat down.

"We now have plans to enter India, we have codenamed it U-Go," informed Terauchi. "I plan to deploy your companies on different posts along the border of Manipur. Their chief assignments will be espionage and propaganda."

"I wish you good luck, Field Marshal," said Bose, "but you have to accept us as your allies. The INA will operate as your equal partners, and will be deployed in not less than a battalion's strength."

Teruschi was reluctant to accept the INA as an ally, so Bose contacted General Sugiyama, the Chief of Staff of the Japanese imperial army, and took his concurrence.

* * * *

The INA's first commitment was the thrust towards Eastern Indian frontiers of Manipur, in close cooperation with Japan. It also started diversionary operations in Arakan province of Burma to confuse the enemy.

While the INA and Japan were gaining ground in Burma and beyond, Bose busied himself in getting support from the friendly nations. He also attended the East Asian Conference, where he was received as the Head of the State, and it was here that Tojo announced to hand over the islands of Andaman and Nicobar to the provisional government of Free India. He also met the emperor of Japan. Besides, he toured Nanjing, Shanghai, Manila, Jakarta, Borneo and Sumatra to widen the scope of his external affairs and gain acceptance.

The Japanese had taken control of Andaman-Nicobar islands in 1942. They allowed Bose to set up the Provisional Government of Free India there. Andaman was renamed Shaheed and Nicobar, Swaraj. Bose visited these islands in early 1944, and appointed Lt. Col. A.D. Loganathan as the Governor General of the islands, but actual administration remained in the hands of the Japanese Navy. Loganathan was disappointed with the frequent Japanese interference in all aspects of administration, so he relinquished the charge and returned to the government's headquarters in Rangoon.

The infamous Cellular Jail was located in Andaman, where the British used to house Indians in the worst form of jail sentence. Known as Kala Pani, it was a dreaded place to undergo imprisonment.

The Indian Tricolour, with the Charkha in the middle stripe, was first hoisted on Indian soil at Moirang, a town in Manipur. The Gandhi and Nehru Brigades of the INA succeeded to lay siege to Kohima and Imphal. The British army retreated suffering a large number of casualties. A large number of defections too took place, boosting the morale of the INA troops despite shortage of rations, medicine, clothing and equipment.

Bose was triumphant at these advances. He went on air and said that now Delhi was not far away. He exhorted the Indians to rise and embrace freedom. He called, "Tum mujhe khoon do, main tumhe azadi doonga." (Give me your blood and I'll give you freedom.)

These evocative words have stuck to the Indian psyche even today.

The INA was making rapid advances, but at the same time, was facing difficulties because the Japanese were facing reversals at other places, and now they were concentrating to defend their core areas and mainland. It was gradually coming under pressure to save its own assets, so it was paying more attention towards its own sustenance and defence, leaving the INA to its fate. On the contrary, the British army was now growing very strong as new recruits from India were joining its ranks and America was cooperating with it completely.

In such precarious times, Bose sought to mint currency and raise taxes on the Indian population living in Malaysia and Singapore. He dreamt of setting up a base in mainland

India at Dimapur or Imphal, but with the defeat of the Japanese army in the Burma War, the INA too had to retreat along with the Japanese army. With this, Bose's dream of expanding hold in mainland India came crashing down with little hope of recovery.

The general withdrawal was ordered, but the British army chased, causing severe damage to Japan and the INA. During the withdrawal, the INA fought a number of battles in Meiktila, Mandalay, Pegu, Yangon and Mount Popa, but reverses could not be prevented. The British air force was causing irreparable damage to the retreating Japanese and INA armies, which were unable to fight back in view of lack of suitable armour and air cover. It came to light that the INA troops were fighting the British tanks with simple rifles and petrol bombs; no one could dream of a victory in such a horrible situation. One thing they did not lack was courage, but they had to retreat from one place to another, and finally, Rangoon too fell. Loganathan surrendered with a large part of the INA. With the loss of Rangoon, the Provisional Government of Free India lost its status of an effective political entity. It withdrew from Rangoon to Singapore, along with the remnants of its brigades and the Rani Jhansi Regiment.

A large number of INA troops died, not from enemy attacks, but from hunger, malaria and rain. They were in a terrible position, and whenever possible, they sought to surrender than run.

The British onslaught on Burma forced Japan to retreat more quickly. The INA too had to retreat. Bose refused to go away alone, he walked with his troops; this march is called an 'epic retreat to safety' by historians, despite the fact that Bose was provided a transport by the Japanese, but not for the INA troops.

Bose reached Singapore in August 1945 with what remained of the INA and his provisional government. The British were pressing and the situation was precarious.

After initial success in East Asia, the INA had been suffering reverses, one after another, though it fought some memorable battles. The British and American troops often wondered how so few men could confront so many enemies so courageously. But by August 1945, several important setbacks had taken place shaking the INA's position in the struggle. The first shock had come a year before when Prime Minister Hideki Tojo had resigned on 22 July, 1944; his descent had diminished support for Bose's mission in the Japanese army, though Bose had some military officers who were trying to help him. Four months ago, Hitler had committed suicide, and it eventually brought Germany under such pressure which could no more be controlled. Bose, however, was confident that he could keep fighting as more and more people were coming in support to his cause, but this time, the Allied forces had become very strong, especially since America had joined their side actively. Whatever little hopes Bose had were crushed on 6 and 9 August, 1945, when America dropped atom bombs on Hiroshima and Nagasaki respectively. The Japanese will to fight the war was decimated completely. Japan announced its intention to surrender on 14

August, 1945, and with this, there was every possibility that if Bose remained in Japan-controlled territory, he could land himself in the British hands.

"I suppose I should go back to India and lead the freedom struggle from there," said Bose.

"No, not in my view, but I think you should consult the cabinet," suggested Subhas.

"Why do you say that?"

"The Indian masses look to you as the only saviour; in the beginning of this movement, they looked at the INA as the agents of the imperialist Japan and fascist forces; now only they have started to see you as the one who is doing something worthwhile for them."

"Japan is losing, so is Italy and Germany. I will, even otherwise, be caught some time later."

"It is difficult to say what lies in the future, but your surrender will bring all these efforts to a complete halt. Maybe you don't realise that they can execute you."

"If they executed me, it would be my supreme sacrifice and it would also ignite the country. I may not free the country alive, but I would certainly do it after my death."

"Netaji, you are growing emotional. You have no right over your life. Let the cabinet take the most considered view," Subhas said bowing low. He wanted to hide the tears that were ready to flow down his eyes, or maybe he was unable to tolerate the wavering state of mind of his favourite Netaji.

"Yes," Bose turned to go saying, "summon the cabinet."

"Don't you think Russia can be a viable option?" Subhas opined.

"Hmm…"

"Whatever your decision, I want to be with you, Netaji," Subhas's throat was choked with emotions, these words fell out of his mouth with a great difficulty.

Bose entered the chamber where his ministers were waiting. They considered all aspects of the prevailing situations and the options they had before them. Finally, it was decided that Bose should go to Russia, only it presented some ray of hope for them.

Russia had helped the Allied Forces in the Second World War, but it was now at loggerheads with Britain and America over its intention of occupying Eastern Europe. There was every possibility that Russia could come to Bose's help, so it was decided that he should leave for Russia; but he could not have reached Russia without Japanese help.

* * * *

The Death

It was 14 August, 1945. Japan had already expressed its intentions to surrender though formal surrender was yet to be held. It had suffered great humiliation and by this surrender it wanted to save all that could be possible.

Bose wanted to go to Russia with his cabinet members, so he contacted Japan's general headquarters but it rejected his proposal. Field Marshal Terauchi was much impressed by Bose; he took personal responsibility for his safe passage.

An aeroplane was arranged that would take Bose and his cabinet members and other persons to Saigon in Vietnam. On the morning of 16 August, 1945, Bose left the Singapore airfield with his comrades. The entire plan was kept confidential.

Bose took his seat in the aeroplane. He said to his comrades: "Today the circumstances may be averse, but we will for sure make them favourable to us. We are flying to Russia to seek its help to reorganise the INA; we are sure to drive the British out of India in a few months. Keep faith that India will be a free nation sooner than later. The journey is still difficult, the path is strewn with several thorns, but our victory is sure to come."

The comrades clapped for their leader. His optimistic attitude had kept them motivated so far. Subhas went on clapping well after all others had stopped.

The aircraft crossed the air limits of Singapore that had been a mute witness to India's freedom struggle. Everybody looked out of the window at the place where they had worked to create history, though without success. Their faces pervaded with emotions, some eyes were damp too.

* * * *

Three hours later, the aeroplane stopped at Bangkok in Thailand for fuel and service. The aeroplane needed some service, it could not fly further, so they had to stay there overnight. Some more INA officers joined them here.

The aeroplane was ready early next morning. Bose and his comrades boarded it. Flying over Cambodia, the aeroplane landed at Saigon for its next stop.

It was about ten in the morning.

As the aeroplane was being refuelled, Bose and his comrades waited at the tarmac. Some of them sat down on the grass near the taxi. They were eager to get out of the Japan-controlled territory, the sooner the better. Their luggage was still in the aeroplane.

Suddenly, some Japanese soldiers arrived on the scene in a one-tonner transport and they started to off-load the luggage from the aeroplane.

"What is this happening?" said Subhas. He was the first to point out.

"Let me find out," said Abid Hasan. He ran to the aeroplane.

"What's the matter, friends?" Abid Hasan addressed the soldiers while trying to bring his breath under control.

"We don't know," said one soldier. "We have been ordered to do it."

The confused Abid walked back to Bose. Just then a Japanese colonel came to them in a jeep. He bowed before Bose and said, "Sir, we are sorry that the aeroplane cannot take off now."

"What's the problem? You may be aware how important it is for me to get out of the territory under your control. The British can capture us any time," Bose said.

"That is right, but we don't have an aeroplane that we can give you now," said the officer.

"This will be like leaving us in the lurch," remarked Bose with anguish.

"I have been instructed to tell you that we are trying to make some arrangement for you. You know Japan is going to surrender, we are very hard pressed," said the officer. "We are making arrangements for your stay here. I hope some aeroplane will be provided to you soon."

* * * *

After the Japanese officer left, Bose and his comrades stood close to each other.

"What do you think must have happened?" said Habib ur Rahman.

"I think our likely association with Russia has perturbed the Japanese," remarked Subhas.

"How can you say that?" asked Abid.

"It is clear like a slate," said Subhas. "If Russia agreed to help us and entered India, Britain would surely be routed because the masses would rise. But then, Russia would have a say in India, and it would pose a threat to the Japanese assets in East Asia."

"Yes, he is right, and his explanations have endeared him to me," said Bose.

"Netaji, what can we do now?" said Abid.

"I think we should wait and watch. Maybe the Japanese will make some arrangements for us to leave," said Bose.

The Japanese soldiers had off-loaded all the luggage on to the one-tonner.

A little later, a Japanese officer came with two jeeps. He saluted Bose and invited him to take a seat in a jeep. He asked other officers to board the jeeps too. Bose took the front seat on the left. Subhas too boarded the first jeep and sat behind Bose. He did not know why he wanted to be close to Bose. He did not want to leave Bose even for a fraction of a second.

The jeeps took them to the officers' mess, located across the airfield's fence, about three km away. The one-tonner had followed them. As they walked in the verandah, they found that it was single officers' accommodation. Bose was accommodated in a room alone. Others were accommodated two in a room each, and Subhas was the last to be accommodated when the officer informed, "I am sorry, I have no more rooms left in this row. I will house you in a room on the back side."

"No problem," said Subhas.

He and the officer walked around the verandah where was located another row of rooms.

"Will you like to have lunch in the room or in the mess?" the officer asked while leaving.

"I don't want to eat," said Subhas looking at the bed which looked quite comfortable. "Better don't disturb me. I want to sleep."

"Okay," said the officer before marching away.

* * * *

There was a knock at the door. Subhas was disturbed from his sleep. He got up and opened the door. The mess boy stood there with a kettle in his hand. "Want tea?"

"Yes," said Subhas.

The boy poured tea into a glass. "What time is it?"

"It is five, Sir," said the boy.

"What are they doing…those people in the front rows?"

"Those guests…they all have gone."

"What…?" Subhas was bewildered. "How can they go away without me?"

He kept the glass on the table and ran. The mess boy was right. All rooms were empty. None of them was there. He stood there stunned for a while, he did not know what to do. He knew he would be in a difficulty if he remained there any more. He saw the mess boy coming towards him. He asked, "Where have they all gone?"

"Two jeeps came and they went away."

"Where did they go?"

"How can I know?" said the mess boy before going towards the mess hall.

He ran out of the mess. Seeing him approaching, the guard at the gate came to attention. "Where have they all gone?"

"Who…the guests?" asked the guard.

"Yes."

"I don't know."

"When did they go?"

"Half an hour ago."

This communication was conducted more by gestures due to the language barrier.

Subhas looked around. He saw the fence across the road. 'Maybe the aeroplane has come,' murmured he to himself.

Just then a jeep came and stopped before the gate. He talked to the guard at the gate, who pointed to Subhas. The jeep had come to take Subhas. He was greatly relieved. He took his seat in the jeep. The driver applied the gear and tried to turn when the engine stopped. The driver turned the key in the ignition, but without success. Despite his best efforts, the jeep could not be started. The guard and Subhas pushed it, but this served no purpose.

"I am sorry, you will have to go on foot," said the driver.

Bose only faintly smiled at the driver and started walking along the fence. The end of the runway became visible a little distance away. He could see an aeroplane parked there. He also saw two jeeps standing close to the aeroplane. He noticed some figures there, but was not sure if they were his comrades. He decided that he must reach there quickly.

With an intention to reach the aeroplane, Subhas walked as fast as he could. He had never felt as nervous as he was feeling now. He had not gone more than two hundred steps when he saw a breach in the wire fence.

'Can I enter from this breach?' Subhas asked himself. 'If I cross the fence from here, the aeroplane will not be more than five hundred yards away, though it is well over three km by the main road. Is there any danger?' He looked around. He didn't find any Japanese guard around. 'This place seems unguarded. I think I can slip into,' decided Subhas.

The breach was not large, but he could enter. He bent forward and taking care of the thorny wire, he stepped in.

"Halt! Who goes there!" a loud voice rang in the air.

The stunned Subhas stood where he was. He couldn't see anyone around, but he raised his hands out of caution. There was no other sound in the atmosphere, he could only hear the sound of the aeroplane's engines that had started.

Seeing no one there, he put his hands down and started to walk towards the runway, when he heard again, "Halt, you intruder!"

This time Subhas could see a Japanese guard emerging out of the trench along the fence on his right. His gun was pointed at him. He had no way but to raise his hands above his head.

"Disclose your identity!" yelled the guard.

"I am Subhas," said he in a nervous tone.

"Who Subhas…? You are an intruder. You don't seem to be a Japanese," the guard screamed at the top of his voice.

"Subhas…I've to go there," Subhas faltered pointing to the aeroplane.

"You liar!" and with this, he fired two rounds.

Subhas was hit on the shoulder and left chest. He fell and in the horizon he could see the aeroplane taking off. His eyes froze where they were.

And a day later, the news about the air crash was doing round in the airfield. The newspapers carried the news of the air crash on 23 August, 1945, and claimed that Subhas Chandra Bose had succumbed to his burns and injuries on 18 August, 1945, a few hours after the crash.

* * * *

In the End

It is a book of historical fiction; however, the circumstances that it deals with are special, hence this writing. Another question arises – Why have I written this work of historical fiction, instead of a research work? Before I answer this question, I think I should first deal into the evidence regarding the death of one of the greatest leaders that India has ever produced: Subhas Chandra Bose. His death is mired in controversy, many still believing that he is alive and will return when the time is ripe for his return. Many are not ready to believe if he ever died, many have raised doubts if the air crash ever occurred, many have also implied the vested interests of several political entities; then what is the truth? What actually happened that resulted into his disappearance? His death has become a myth. Several times people have said that he will appear, but it has not happened. And now, Bose, if alive, would have been aged well over twelve decades. I have a theory about his disappearance and until I can prove it, let us take the entire story as fiction. For now, let me first deal with the evidence and popular concepts.

Why People Think Bose Didn't Die

On a few occasions before, Bose had disappeared all of a sudden and reappeared at a different time and a different place pursuing a mission in the service of the motherland; the most famous disappearance was in 1941 when he disappeared from his house arrest and people in India later came to know about his presence in Germany. And then he was to disappear in Germany to reappear in Southeast Asia in 1943. When his death was reported in an air crash in 1945, people thought that he had not died and was after some noble goal. These appearances and disappearances made him a legend in his life time, and the myth of his being alive has lived on.

How can it be possible that no photograph was taken of the injured or deceased Bose in hospital, though he occupied a very high position as the Head of the State of the Provisional Government of Free India and was well within the territory of the favourable territory of Japanese empire? Even otherwise, he was a popular person among Japanese and Indians. Even his officers were not shown a dead body, nor was a death certificate ever issued. The INA officers continued to believe that he was in either China, or Japan, or Russia. Reports also came that he was sighted in Calcutta and Siberia. Others believed that he became a Sanyasi (recluse) and went in the Himalayas to undertake penance; he had in his youth shown inclination for this.

Gumnami Baba: There has been a mysterious person in India known as Gumnami Baba. The name signifies 'A Saint with Lost Name' or 'Unknown Old Man'. He lived in Faizabad, a town in Uttar Pradesh. He shared several physical similarities with Subhas Chandra Bose; moreover, he was also found in possession of several items that presumably belonged to Bose. After his death, from his possession were found some articles presumably Netaji's, which he had managed to acquire somehow. The articles included binoculars, photographs of two postage stamps, some letters, some newspaper cuttings, a handmade map of Bangladesh, a telegram from Calcutta, the book *Himalayan Blunder* with notes and a letter from M.S. Golwalkar (Guruji) of the Rashtriya Swayamsevak Sangh (RSS).

The talk is ripe that he was Bose himself, but this is not the truth, as per me. My study points out that he was just a lookalike, who happened to be with Bose for some time, and came to possess some of his articles when Bose was fleeing Singapore. He remained completely tight-lipped about himself; actually, he could not have said anything, because he himself was not the great leader. There is no wonder that doppelgangers are found in the world.

Let us tell you that Gumnami Baba died in 1985 at Faizabad and he was cremated by the government authorities in a secret manner.

Statement by Col. Habib ur Rahman

Col. Habib ur Rahman is said to have accompanied Bose in his last flight, and later submitted a statement about Netaji's death that he saw him dying with his own eyes, but it could not be proved. Let us not forget that there are doubts whether he was in the same aeroplane in which Bose had to travel. The points which make his credentials suspicious are many. He has remained tight-lipped; he later joined Pakistan and fought against India. His statement about the plane crash has not been convincing. Moreover, Mukherjee Commission has cast aspersions about the veracity of his statement.

Enquiry Commissions and Committees

After independence, at the entreaty of countrymen, the Government of India, in 1956, appointed a four-member committee, under the chairmanship of Shah Nawaz Khan, then a Member of Parliament and formerly a Lieutenant Colonel in the INA, to look into the facts of Subhas Chandra Bose's death. This committee also comprised Suresh Chandra Bose, an elder brother of Bose. This committee visited Japan, Thailand and Vietnam in addition to a few places in India and interviewed all survivors of the plane crash as well some other witnesses. It also interviewed Habib ur Rahman, said to accompany Bose on the flight. Those days, India did not have good diplomatic relations with Taiwan, so the government there did not cooperate in the matter. Of the total three committee members, Khan and Maitra concluded that Bose had died in the air crash, but Suresh Chandra

Bose gave a dissenting note as there were discrepancies in the witnesses and evidence. He noted that crucial evidence had been withheld from him and that Jawaharlal Nehru had directed the committee to infer that the death had occurred in the air crash.

In 1970, the Government of India appointed a new one-man commission, under the chairmanship of G.D. Khosla, a retired high court judge. He concurred with the earlier findings as noted by Shah Nawaz Committee.

The myth of Bose being alive was further asserted by Mukherjee Commission, appointed by the Government of India under the chairmanship of Justice Mukherjee, in 2005. It examined the available evidence for six years from 1999 to 2005 and prepared a report in cooperation with the Taiwanese government. This committee submitted its report on 8 November, 2005. It submitted that, according to the Taiwanese government account, no such air crash had occurred at Taipei on 18 August, 1945, in which Bose was travelling. The report also concluded that there seemed to be a secret plan to ensure Bose's safe passage to the USSR with the knowledge of the Japanese authorities and Habib ur Rahman.

Some information filtered in from American department which supported the Taiwanese account. The American sources revealed that no air crash had occurred during the given period. It is clear that Bose did not die in the air crash. The remains kept at Renkō-ji temple in Japan, which are claimed to be Bose's, are not his either.

According to my theory, he died of course, but not in the air crash, nor in Japanese/Russian/Chinese captivity. Had he lived, there was no reason he could have remained in hiding this long. He did not contact Emilie even, which further strengthens my theory. The above findings and evidence are quite contradictory and only support my theory. This theory can be further proved if a DNA test is carried out of the ashes kept at the Buddhist Temple at Renkō-ji.

Thank you.

– **A.K. Gandhi**